THE EARHART MISSION

Denis Keyser: He's a reporter with a chance for the story of a lifetime—but this time, the price is too high.

Colonel Stanley Cerilla: The Pentagon's man, he's responsible for keeping *the secret*, and he's authorized to go to any length to do so.

Peter Sloan: A college professor who's specialized in Amelia Earhart's past, he knows a great deal—perhaps too much.

Jason Caldwell: He's just made a killing on Wall Street, and he's itching to do it again—this time in the South Seas.

Peggy Allenby: Caldwell's voluptuous young mistress, on this trip she discovers she needs more from him than just love.

Emily Stenemond: A little old lady from Australia, it's her incredible claim that sparks a globe-spanning search for a long-lost treasure.

THE EARHART MISSION

Peter Tanous

BANTAM BOOKS
TORONTO · NEW YORK · LONDON · SYDNEY

THE EARHART MISSION

*A Bantam Book / published by arrangement with
Simon & Schuster*

PRINTING HISTORY

Simon & Schuster edition published January 1980

The excerpt from Winged Legend, *by John Burke, published in 1970
by Berkley Medallion Books, a division of G. P. Putnam's Sons, is
used by permission.*

The excerpt from the poem "Courage Is the Price," from Last Flight
*by Amelia Earhart, published in 1937 by Harcourt Brace Jovanovich,
Inc., is used by permission.*

Bantam edition / August 1982

ISBN 0-553-20943-4

Published simultaneously in the United States and Canada

PRINTED IN THE UNITED STATES OF AMERICA

O   0 9 8 7 6 5 4 3 2 1

To ROSE
and JOE,
and ANN

Prologue

The old woman entered the waiting room and quietly sat down. The ache in her spine was worse now and she hoped the doctor might finally do something to relieve her agony. He had held out some hope at the last session, a veiled reference to some new techniques for relieving pain. Normally, Emily Stenemond would be wary of novel medical treatments, but Dr. Wilton had a solid reputation as one of the finest physicians in Australia.

A nurse turned to the old lady and smiled cheerfully. "Dr. Wilton will see you now, ma'am."

She tendered her hand to help Mrs. Stenemond to her feet but the woman ignored the gesture and rose under her own power.

Dr. James C. Wilton greeted his patient, then listened while Mrs. Stenemond described once more the piercing pain that afflicted her, from the base of the neck to the buttocks. It came in spurts, but a residual ache was always present.

Dr. Wilton nodded. "I think the time has come to try a different approach," he said.

Mrs. Stenemond sat silently while her doctor unveiled his plan for a cure. "We have so far tried every known test applicable to your symptoms," Wilton continued. "All of the results are negative. That is, they show no sign of bone damage or muscular strain. The exercises I prescribed, although fitting for a woman of your age, have not helped either."

Mrs. Stenemond focused her full attention on the physician, but her face betrayed no emotion.

"What I propose, Mrs. Stenemond, is hypnosis. It could help in two ways. Pains that cannot otherwise be diagnosed are sometimes caused by psychosomatic trauma. The patient is not aware of the causes—at least not consciously. Under hypnosis, the subconscious will often release the true symptoms and we can then proceed with a cure. In other cases, a clue may be discovered by reaching back in one's memory to a forgotten incident that may have started the problem, like a fall or an accident of some sort. Such information can help us localize the source of the problem."

"I . . . I don't know . . ." Mrs. Stenemond said, her voice hesitant.

"I assure you, there is neither danger nor aftereffect. I have spent eight months in Munich studying the techniques of hypnotic analysis so I am well qualified to administer the therapy. In any event, I am afraid it is all I have to offer."

The old woman bit her lower lip as a new attack of pain ripped through her body. She closed her eyes, trying not to cry out. Soon the pain subsided and she gazed at her physician. "I'll try whatever you suggest," she said.

Dr. Wilton led his patient to an adjoining room and sat her on a couch. When he knew she was comfortable, he began to induce the trance. He spoke softly, the words flowing easily in a soft exhortation to sleep, a rhythmic succession of carefully chosen thoughts and sounds.

In minutes, the trance was induced.

"Mrs. Stenemond? Can you hear me?"

"Yes," came the reply. But the woman did not look at her doctor. Her eyes seemed to take in a vision that only she could see.

"Do you feel pain?"

"No. Not now."

"Can you remember when your back pains first began?"

"Yes. It was in the plane crash."

The reply puzzled Wilton. Mrs. Stenemond had never before mentioned a plane crash.

"When did this crash occur?" Wilton asked.

"Long ago." Mrs. Stenemond's voice became agitated. "I cannot stay here very long. I must go."

"Go where?"

Silence.

"Mrs. Stenemond?"

She did not respond.

"Mrs. Stenemond?" Wilton called again, this time in a louder voice.

"Why do you call me by that name?" Mrs. Stenemond asked.

"Because it is your name."

The old woman shook her head. "My name is Amelia Earhart."

part ONE

chapter

1

The clatter and hum of the New York *Daily Press*'s newsroom signaled the end of the day and the inexorable approach of another deadline.

As he always did, Buddy Levine, a thin, blue-jean-clad copyboy, scanned the various newswires while he walked by the machines. He stopped in front of the Reuters wire and read the story spewing out in rapid spurts. Buddy cradled the cans of Coke under his arm and held the wire copy up with his free hand.

"Hey, Denis!" Buddy shouted across the newsroom. "Have a look at this!"

Denis Keyser peered over a row of desks to where Buddy was waving. The young reporter rose and crumpled the piece of copy he had just read. He took careful aim at a wastepaper basket three desks away, pumped once for practice, then let the wad of paper fly, scoring easily. He added two points to his lifetime total, now in the thousands, and headed toward the newswires. Denis had developed an easygoing friendship with the copyboy, who was grateful for the time Denis took to explain some of the tricks of news reporting to him and for the occasional sharing of their sandwich lunch when payday was a distant memory. In return,

Buddy Levine saw to it that his friend Denis was never without a needed soft drink and, of course, Denis was always the first to learn of an important story coming over the wires.

"What's up?" Denis asked.

"Don't ask. Look," Buddy said excitedly. He handed over a can of Coke while Denis read the copy.

"I'll be damned . . ." Denis tore the copy off the machine and read while he walked slowly back to his desk.

MAY 21—REUTERS—SYDNEY, AUSTRALIA—A.M. LEAD ** 1310 ** An Australian physician, Dr. James C. Wilton, claimed today that one of his patients, Mrs. Emily Stenemond, of Sydney, believes that she is the missing aviatrix Amelia Earhart.

Mrs. Stenemond, 78, had sought treatment of an undisclosed ailment. At a press conference, Dr. Wilton said he tried hypnosis after traditional remedies had failed. While under a trance, Mrs. Stenemond identified herself as Amelia Earhart and recounted various aspects of the famous aviatrix's life and exploits.

According to Wilton, she spoke of Earhart's last voyage and referred to a "Project Sherman," which could not be immediately associated with any of Miss Earhart's known exploits. When not under a trance, Mrs. Stenemond denied any knowledge of Miss Earhart or her possible identity with the American air pioneer.

-o-

When he had finished reading, Denis sat down and stretched luxuriously. His imagination had been uncharacteristically caught by the story. He shared the cynical nature of most reporters, a nature strengthened by growing up in a rough section of the Bronx where you respected the Golden Gloves before the Golden Rule. But he recognized in the Amelia Earhart dispatch the makings of a big story, and in the newspaper business, you were promoted, and more importantly, paid for big stories.

Stretching again, this time to peer over his colleagues'

heads, Denis saw that Herb Latelle, the Press's assignment editor, who sat across the newsroom in a glass-paneled office, was no longer on the phone. Denis rose and walked briskly to Latelle's office, hoping to get there before the phone rang again.

Latelle didn't bother to look up when his young colleague stepped into his sanctuary, knowing somehow that the visitor was a lesser mortal, at least in the paper's particular pecking order. The wrinkles in the editor's face had deepened with time to seem more like scars, his battle ribbons for forty years at the *Daily Press*. The phone rang again, as if on cue, providing Latelle with another opportunity to display priorities. A phone call was invariably more important than a young reporter, even one who had been a Nieman fellow. Long ago, Latelle had taken upon himself the heroic task of keeping those wet-behind-the-ears juniors in their place, all in the name of good journalistic training.

Denis understood Latelle's game and smiled fatalistically. They had warned him at the Columbia School of Journalism that every newspaper in the country had a Herb Latelle who could make or break a young journalist's career.

The phone slammed down and Latelle looked up. "That son of a bitch Cummings wants a week off. Do you believe that? A political reporter wants time off just before the primaries?"

"It might have something to do with his wedding," Denis said laconically.

"Did I tell him to get married the week before the primaries? Did I? This is no college newspaper, you know. You fuckin' college guys treat your job like an interlude between campus mixers." Latelle picked up a Camel and lit it. He looked at Denis, frowned at his appearance, and asked: "What do you want?"

"The Amelia Earhart story. A Reuters report just came in over the wire that a woman in Sydney says she's Amelia Earhart. I want to follow it up."

Latelle gazed at the ceiling in a moment of concentration, then looked back at Denis. "Fine. Do it. Good-bye."

"There's one thing," Denis continued. "To do it right, I'll have to travel."

"Sure, Keyser, sure. Here's a token. Take the IRT to Forty-second Street, walk two blocks east to the library, okay? Now, the rest of us have a deadline to meet, so if you don't mind . . ."

"Wait a second, Herb," Denis said in an exasperated voice, "that woman is in Australia. I've got to talk to her, her doctor, friends—"

"Australia? You gotta be kidding." A mock smile came over Latelle's weatherbeaten face as he aimed a pencil in deadly earnest at Denis. "You know something, Keyser, twenty minutes ago a guy came in here about a story in Trenton. You know what I told him? I said use the fucking telephone! After five! So I'll tell you what. I'll authorize two phone calls to Australia, okay? Keep 'em short."

Denis walked out of the office, his lips pursed, his fists clenched. He was barely through the door before a feeling of shame washed over him. When he was ten his friends called him chicken when he'd run away from a bigger boy, sobbing as he fled. That feeling and memory rarely returned, but when it did it sickened him.

Denis stopped, turned on his heel, and marched back into Latelle's office. He took a deep breath and felt the blood rushing to his face. He chose his words carefully. "Herb, you are a first-class son of a bitch."

Latelle looked up with an expression of utter incredulity.

Denis continued, carefully controlling his voice. "It's not just your narrow-minded, asinine attitude about this story. I can live with that. But, Herb, I've been working for this goddamn newspaper for five years and I'm not putting up with any more of your shit."

"Are you finished?" Latelle hissed.

"Up yours, Herb," Denis said, and walked out, without waiting for a reply.

When he returned to his desk, several colleagues who had heard the exchange looked toward Denis and smiled.

16

Some gave the V sign, others feigned applause, and the one black reporter in the newsroom snapped a flashy closed fist in the black-power salute. Through his glass wall, Denis saw that Latelle was still shaking his head, and he wondered if he detected a thin smile forming on the old man's lips.

The young reporter left the newsroom and headed for the morgue, the newspaper's research library. Denis had thick brown hair and a masculine face whose features were appropriate to a fairly handsome thirty-year-old man. A tall, trim body and conditioned fitness made Denis walk with the confident gait of an athlete. His deep blue eyes reflected the determination of a young man who had withstood the hardships of a childhood in the South Bronx, and ignored a possible crack at a professional basketball contract, to pursue a different kind of career in a field he loved: journalism. The word still had a magic ring. To Denis, it meant something far deeper than seeing one's by-line in print. Journalism was the transubstantiation of the First Amendment, the living witness to freedom of speech, the vehicle for seeking out the truth, no matter whom it might affect. Denis' parents, although justifiably proud of him, had nurtured a secret hope that their talented son might devote his unflagging energy to a field whose rewards were less ephemeral and more practical, so that future generations of Keysers might be free from the oppression of a squalid New York borough. Denis, who adored his parents, was sensitive to this potential failing, and he often fantasized about striking it rich. But so far, his only effort in that direction was the weekly purchase of a ticket in the New York State Lottery.

Denis counted on spending a couple of hours in the morgue, which wasn't too bad except for one thing: Cissy Durham, a former secretary with impressive physical dimensions, who had been banished there to keep the newspaper clippings in order and to keep her from disrupting impressionable reporters' deadlines. Cissy still pursued Denis in a manner which transcended the blunt and bordered on the crude.

"Hi, gorgeous," Cissy said when she saw Denis approach

her counter. Her shoulder-length auburn hair coiffed a decent-enough face that would have rated a five on a scale of ten for those who kept that kind of score. Her body earned much higher points.

Denis smiled at her. "I've got a big job, Cis."

Cissy smiled back and leaned over the counter, a studied gesture that accentuated the size of her breasts. Denis made a point of looking the other way. Behind them lay the morgue, the repository of clippings dating back to the year the paper was founded, ten years before the turn of the century. Along the walls of the huge room, rows of dilapidated filing cabinets were strung out, surrounding a bank of desks where two older men clipped articles for filing and another arranged them in the cabinets. On the right-hand side of the room, the "clips" were organized by subject and by name, while on the facing side, a similar grouping of photographs was stored away for reference. The poor lighting reflected the dinginess of the surroundings.

"Do you think we'll ever get this place out of the Middle Ages?" Denis sighed. Most other papers had converted their morgues to computer retrieval systems, or at the very least, microfiche film records. But not the Press. Here, you fingered through the filing cabinets for the clips you needed or, if you were lucky, Cissy did it for you. In Denis' case, Cissy was more than happy to oblige.

"I need everything you've got on Amelia Earhart," Denis stated. He filled out the request slip and left the dates blank.

Cissy undulated over to the name files and retrieved several manila envelopes with the Earhart name in the upper corner followed by the relevant dates.

"What do I get for my trouble?" Cissy asked playfully.

"How about lunch one day?" Denis replied, figuring he had picked a safe reward.

"I'd prefer 'funch.' " Cissy grinned.

"I'm afraid to ask . . ."

"Figure it out, sport." Cissy turned and headed to the files.

Denis settled in at one of the reading tables. The top envelope yielded a stack of clippings on Earhart from the mid-thirties. The date was stamped on top of each clip. He organized them by month and began to read.

The first significant mention of Miss Earhart was in connection with a flight she made in June 1928, as the first woman to cross the Atlantic in an airplane. Another article offered a rambling background piece on how Amelia had been chosen for the flight. The financial backer of the project, a wealthy socialite, had insisted that the woman chosen be "of the right image."

Denis chuckled at the snobbery of it all. He glanced over at the morgue's counter, where Cissy was leaning, her posterior prominently protruding. Honey, Denis thought, you would never have made it.

After an hour and a half, Denis replaced all of the clippings in their respective envelopes and returned them to the desk. He shoved several pages of handwritten notes in his pocket.

"Hey, Cissy!" Denis called into the file room.

Cissy responded in a flash. "What can I do for you, chum?"

"Now I need what you've got on anyone claiming to be Amelia Earhart since 1937 and also anything by the name of Project Sherman. Go back to the mid-thirties on that one, please."

Cissy grumbled something about work and life in general and proceeded to the filing cabinets. Her mission took less than fifteen minutes.

"Here's the stuff on the Earhart claims," she said, handing Denis two more envelopes. "Most of it is from the sixties and seventies. As far as your Project Sherman is concerned, the only thing I could find is about a battle tank."

"Thanks, Cissy," Denis said, and began to attack the envelopes. As he read along, he found the stories of the Earhart incarnations almost as interesting as the aviatrix's true-life story. Here and there, a woman claimed to be, or was identified as, Amelia Earhart, a woman who, the story went, had escaped the fatal crash, was taken prisoner by the Japanese, and finally reemerged in a new identity in California, or Utah, or New Jersey. Often, a follow-up story provided all the evidence needed to disprove the original claim.

Denis read the story of the Utah woman with great interest. Here was a housewife who could scarcely remember her youth but who ventured into a Piper Cub one day and found herself flying the machine effortlessly, although she had never had a flying lesson in her life. She was in her mid-seventies, and suddenly people discovered a certain physical resemblance to the great heroine herself. As he read the story, Denis skimmed over the part dealing with the investigation of the allegations; then suddenly something caught his eye. He retraced his visual steps until he read: "Colonel Stanley Cerilla." He had seen that name before. Looking back through the stack of clippings he had already examined, Denis discovered Colonel Cerilla's name again, this time at the scene of another Amelia Earhart look-alike. In little time, Denis found Cerilla's name in three more Earhart incarnation stories. Interesting, Denis thought. He wrote the colonel's name on his notepaper for further reference.

Another name cropped up in the articles, but only twice. Dr. Peter Sloan, of Georgetown University, was frequently interviewed in connection with the history of the Far East at the time Amelia Earhart disappeared. He offered his own theory that Miss Earhart was engaged in some sort of government mission when she was lost. Another name for further reference, Denis thought.

Working carefully, the young reporter stuffed the clippings back into their respective envelopes, and, against all rules, prepared to take them home with him. He worried about what it might cost him if Cissy spotted their removal.

She did. Just as Denis was about to go through the door.

"Naughty, naughty!" Cissy chided, but she was smiling.

Denis gave her a winning grin. "Gotta do some research at home, Cis. I'll have the stuff back on Monday, okay?"

"Well . . ."

"Hey, Cis. About lunch . . ."

"I didn't say 'lunch.' "

"I know. I figured it out."

"When, Denis?"

"I'll be thinking about it all weekend, Cis. Thanks."

Denis breathed a sigh of relief and hurried back to the newsroom. It wasn't that Cissy was unattractive, but to Denis her bold, animal pursuit techniques took all the fun away. Besides, he was emotionally committed to just one woman, whose number he proceeded to dial as soon as he arrived at his desk.

The phone answered on the third ring. "Sacha?" Denis said. He loved saying her name. She was the first Sacha he had ever met, or for that matter, ever heard of. She was a strikingly beautiful, lissome model with blond hair and delicate features, who adored Denis to the exclusion of other potential, far wealthier suitors.

"I can't make it tonight," Denis said, allowing her disappointment to settle before he continued. "I've got a new assignment. The Amelia Earhart story. You'll hear about it on the news tonight. I need to do some research, fast."

"When will I see you, Denis?" said the lilting, disappointed voice.

"We'll get together Friday night. I'll tell you about it then."

chapter
2

The telephone call from Captain Hilton Railey had been straightforward enough. Would Amelia be willing to be a candidate for a flight across the Atlantic? Without skipping a beat, she replied that she would. Thereafter, a rigorous selection process ensued. Amelia Earhart would appear before a select panel brought together by the flight's backer, wealthy socialite Mrs. Frederick Guest. The dual purpose of the flight would be to serve Anglo-American solidarity and allow, for the first time, a woman to cross the Atlantic in an airplane. Because of the historic importance of the flight, Mrs. Guest insisted that the American girl chosen be "of the right image."

At first sight of her, Hilton Railey was certain that Amelia was his candidate. She was twenty-nine, shy, modest, and had a winning smile. Moreover, she looked enough like Charles Lindbergh to be his sister.

Amelia appeared before the all-male panel in the spring of 1928. She fielded their questions deftly and later reflected: "If they did not like me at all ... I would be deprived of the trip. If they liked me too well, they might be loath to drown me. It was, therefore, necessary for me to maintain an attitude of impenetrable mediocrity."

A few days later, Amelia received a letter saying she had been selected for the flight. Unlike the two male crew members, she would receive no pay. Her only reward, if they made it, would be the fame attendant on the first woman to fly the Atlantic.

To most military men, an assignment to the Pentagon ranks high on the list of desirable posts, the kind of tour you earn as a reward for demonstrable excellence in places like Korea or Fort Benning, Georgia, where nobody but the Army's fanatic fringe wants to be stationed. Colonel Stanley Cerilla, U.S. Army, could boast of both competence and luck. Following two earlier tours in Korea, Cerilla was transferred to Military Intelligence in Washington, where, over a period of fourteen years, he had carved out a niche for himself in the intelligence field and had acquired a reputation as an officer who could be entrusted with some of the country's most sensitive secrets. In the process, Cerilla had ensured his continued tenure at the Pentagon.

At forty-eight, Colonel Cerilla was the recruiting-poster image of the military officer. His direct eyes, square jaw, and graying hair invoked the kind of confidence that soldiers seek in their field commanders. But despite his on-the-job qualities, some of his colleagues found Cerilla a bore, a one-dimensional, career-oriented soldier who had few outside interests. He had married early and was widowed early, and chose never again to expose himself to the emotional suffering he had endured when his young wife died.

Cerilla was reading the Washington Post when his deputy, Captain John Turner, walked up to the colonel's gray metal desk, a news dispatch in his hand.

"Another Amelia Earhart story, Colonel," Turner said, handing over the paper.

"Well, I guess it was due," Cerilla commented with a wry smile. "I haven't had one to work with in almost two years."

"Yes, sir, since the woman in Utah. That was just another fake story. I'm not so sure about this one, though."

"They're all the same, Captain." Cerilla yawned. "I ought to know. I've investigated seventeen of them so far."

"I'm afraid this case is really different, sir," Turner insisted. "This woman in Australia has referred to Project Sherman."

Cerilla stared incredulously at the young officer. He picked up the dispatch and read it carefully. As he finished, a frown appeared on his brow, and, ignoring Turner's presence, he pushed the intercom button. "Letty, I want you to get through to the Secretary's office. Tell them I need to see the Secretary as soon as possible. If it's necessary, you may tell them it's urgent."

At precisely 1:45 P.M. Colonel Cerilla was shown into the office of the Secretary of Defense. The Secretary, who had been in office only two months, was a popular chief at the Pentagon. Although he had dabbled in politics for a number of years, he had served three years as Secretary of the Army, under a prior Democratic administration, and he knew and understood the intricacies of the job. His mild and courteous manner enhanced his reputation with those Defense Department employees who did not subscribe to the theory that military men must be gruff and surly to be respected.

The Secretary showed Cerilla to the brown leather sofa in the corner of his office. Once Cerilla was settled, the senior official took a notepad and a sharpened pencil and sat on a nearby leather armchair. As Cerilla prepared to speak, the flag of the Department of Defense, standing alongside the Stars and Stripes behind the massive desk, reminded him of the importance of the conversation that was about to begin.

"Mr. Secretary, may I start by saying that I would not have bothered you if I did not earnestly believe that the subject I will discuss deserves the highest level of attention and briefing."

The Secretary smiled understandingly. "I'm quite sure of that, Colonel."

Cerilla summed up the recent developments concerning the woman who claimed to be Amelia Earhart. "Yes, I read about that this morning in my newspaper summary," the Secretary acknowledged.

"The woman spoke of a Project Sherman," Cerilla continued, "which lends credibility to her claim. I thought I should brief you on Project Sherman."

Cerilla then revealed to his superior the details of one of the Pentagon's most closely guarded secrets. Although the fact is still not recorded in most modern histories of the United States, the American government in 1937 granted a secret loan of 100 million dollars to the Chinese government of Chiang Kai-shek. Its purpose was to help the Chinese wage their war with Japan over Manchuria. The ill-equipped Chinese army was being slaughtered at the hands of the vicious, and better supplied, Japanese forces. At the time, the U.S. government was gravely concerned about the expansionist policy of the Japanese, and many American experts advised President Roosevelt that it was only a matter of time before the Japanese attacked the United States. The money would help China fight Japan, and thus head off the possibility of the Japanese attacking the United States.

"If the Japanese knew about the loan," Cerilla continued, "it could have provided them with the excuse they needed to attack us. But that wasn't the only reason for secrecy."

"What else, Colonel?"

"The country was still in the Depression of 1937, so any kind of foreign loan would have been politically embarrassing to an awful lot of congressmen. The President did let two Cabinet officers and a few congressional leaders in on the secret, but, I suppose, only because he needed their help and approval."

The loan was to be made in gold, which was not unusual for those times and circumstances, and the problem of delivering it was given to the Secretary of War. An American destroyer, the USS *Sherman*, was scheduled to leave San Francisco for Howland Island, in the South Pacific, in early

June, and it would be a relatively simple matter to load the gold on the ship, in a sealed compartment, and, once the *Sherman* was at Howland, transmit special secret instructions to the captain to proceed to Shanghai. The Chinese would be notified of the ship's arrival date so they could arrange for the unloading of the precious cargo.

From time to time, the Secretary made notes, but mostly he just listened. The door opened and a uniformed orderly entered, a telex in his hand. The Secretary waved him off and invited Cerilla to continue.

Everything went according to plan until the *Sherman* left Howland on June 20, 1937. Two days later, all communications with the ship ceased. After several days of silence from the *Sherman*, the President and other officials who knew about the cargo were in a quandary. The Japanese allowed no overflights of the mandated islands, and any aerial reconnaissance attempt to find the *Sherman* would inevitably include Japanese-held territory.

"So the ship was lost," the Secretary commented, stroking his chin.

"Yes, sir," Cerilla continued, "and that left President Roosevelt in a ... well, ticklish situation. There was a hundred million dollars in American gold on that ship, which we could ill afford to give up."

"We could ill afford it today," the Secretary added wryly.

Cerilla smiled and picked up the story. "We don't know which one of Roosevelt's aides finally came up with the idea, but one of them reminded the President that Amelia Earhart was going to be in that general area within a few days as she completed her round-the-world flight. Well, FDR and Mrs. Roosevelt happened to be friendly with Amelia and her publisher husband, George Putnam, so here was an opportunity the President couldn't pass up. As with most of his decisions, the President made this one quickly."

As soon as he had finished the last sentence, Cerilla hoped the Secretary would not take his comment as a criticism of the current White House occupant, whose decision-making faculties were slow and ponderous.

Cerilla continued, accelerating the pace of his narrative for fear of taking too much of the Secretary's time. Once FDR's decision had been made, a special presidential emissary, John Latham, was dispatched to Port Darwin in Australia to meet with Amelia Earhart, who would be landing there on her round-the-world flight. They met on June 27, 1937, and Latham spoke with her for two full days, causing a stopover delay that subsequently puzzled many followers of Amelia's flight, and which has never been publicly explained. Latham told Amelia the full story of the *Sherman* mission and finally convinced her that the only hope of finding the ship was a special aerial reconnaissance by her aircraft, the only flight that would not arouse Japanese hostilities. Amelia agreed to the mission after reading the handwritten note from FDR urging her to do so. Shortly thereafter, Fred Noonan, Amelia's navigator, was informed of the decision, and he accepted it calmly.

"I know I've taken up a good deal of your time already, Mr. Secretary," Cerilla remarked solicitously. "Would you prefer I finish later?"

"Heavens no, Colonel! This is one helluva story. I'm surprised it's never leaked out of here."

Cerilla allowed a thin smile. "We manage to keep some secrets, sir. This one, and several others, are known to only a handful of officers. The senior officer—in this case, myself—has the responsibility of briefing the Secretary of Defence, who then decides if it will remain classified. So far, all of your predecessors have chosen to keep the *Sherman* story under wraps."

"I think I can guess why, Colonel, but do continue."

"Yes, sir. We were at the point where Miss Earhart agreed to search for the *Sherman*. Well, according to plan, on the flight from Lae to Howland, Amelia veered off her original route and began the search in the general area indicated to her by John Latham. Shortly thereafter, she radioed, on a special secret frequency, that she had sighted floating debris from a shipwreck, including several survivors who were drifting on anything that would float. She indicated that she was running low on fuel, and broke off communication before she could give her position. Then she must have tried to reach Howland, but when the radio was heard again, Amelia was clearly lost. In those days, navigation equipment was poor."

"I know there has always been a lot of speculation that Amelia Earhart was on some kind of government mission."

"Yes, sir. But most speculation had it that she was to overfly the mandated islands to see if the Japanese were fortifying them. Those who held this point of view were only half right. Amelia was indeed on a government mission, but not for the reasons so frequently advanced."

The Secretary nodded and took a few more notes. Then he said: "I presume there were search parties and whatnot to find Earhart's plane."

"Oh, yes. Scores of Navy vessels and carrier planes participated in the search, but none of them dared venture into Japanese airspace or the coastal areas of the mandated islands. So her plane was never found, and frankly, we don't know what happened to it."

"What about the *Sherman?*"

"That was never found either. The President considered ordering a search-and-salvage attempt, but there was always the problem of the Japanese. The *Sherman* would not have intentionally strayed into Japanese waters, but who knows? In any event, no one knew exactly where the ship went down."

"You mentioned, Colonel, that Amelia Earhart said she saw some survivors."

"Yes, sir. There were fifteen known survivors of the *Sherman* disaster, all young sailors who had no knowledge of the ship's mission or cargo. They were picked up, in varying states of health, by the British who were garrisoned in the Gilbert Islands nearby. Most of them had been floating on debris for several days, and only their youth and good physical condition allowed them to survive."

"Well, didn't any of them know what happened?" The Secretary's voice displayed a touch of annoyance.

"No, sir. All of the survivors were thoroughly debriefed by military intelligence, and not one of them knew what hit him. They assumed they were struck by a torpedo."

"What about the ship's location?"

"No clues. None of them had any idea. But that's not surprising, since most of them were below deck at the time. And the currents in the area are irregular, so we couldn't even come close to retracing the survivors' paths."

The Secretary looked at his watch and frowned. "I'll be late for an appointment at the White House. What are the implications of what you've told me, Colonel?"

"Well, Mr. Secretary, the first point is that the woman in Australia mentioned Project Sherman, so, as strange as it may sound, we've got to accept the possibility that she may be Amelia Earhart."

"That would certainly be interesting. What else?"

"The gold, Mr. Secretary. If she is genuine, sooner or later she'll tell about the Sherman mission and the gold on that ship. Incidentally, at today's prices the value of the Sherman's cargo is close to a half billion dollars."

"A half billion?"

"Yes, sir. We were lending the Chinese one hundred million dollars in gold at 1937 prices. It's worth a lot more now. If this woman reveals the secret of the Sherman, it will start a scramble to find the wreck."

"Well, why haven't the Chinese tried to find it sooner?"

"For the same reason we haven't, sir. No one knows where the ship went down."

"But, of course, this woman—the Australian—if she is Amelia Earhart, she'll also know the location of the ship."

"Precisely. And that information could easily be drawn out in one of her hypnotic trances and subsequently get printed in every newspaper in the world."

"All right, Colonel. I've got the picture. I'll try to get a private minute with the President later and mention this to him. I've known him a long time, you know, and I'm pretty sure I know how he'll react."

"How's that, sir, if I may ask?"

The Secretary grinned as he gathered some papers on his desk to take with him to the Cabinet meeting. "He won't want anyone but the United States getting hold of that American gold. We're not about to play 'Treasure Hunt' with the rest of the world for our own property." The Secretary mulled over his own words for a few seconds, then continued in a serious tone. "Colonel Cerilla, one of the more dangerous things you've told me is that we've got a forty-year-old cover-up on our hands. As much as I hate to be a part of it, this goddamn cover-up is going to have to go on a little while longer. Now, I want you to work full-time on this project. Report directly to me. Who's your commanding officer? It's General Stratton, isn't it? I'll have a word with him in the morning."

As the two men walked out of the office into the Secretary's anteroom, Cerilla said, "I expect the press will zero in on the Earhart story, sir. It's possible some of them may come to the Pentagon for comment. Those inquiries are automatically referred to me."

"Well, remember, Colonel—say 'No comment' if you have to, but don't lie. If the Earhart cover-up ever gets out, I don't want this administration embarrassed by official false statements. The country's had enough of those to last a hundred years, or until the Republicans get back in, whichever comes first."

chapter
3

Four years had passed since Amelia's transatlantic flight had propelled her to worldwide fame, but a feeling of frustration came over her. Having in fact crossed the Atlantic as a passenger, Amelia did not feel that she deserved her publicity-generated reputation as the premier woman flier in the world. She felt strongly that to earn her fame, she must fly the Atlantic alone.

After months of preparation, including a course in meteorology and long hours of practice at blind flying, Amelia was ready to take the Lockheed, equipped with a new 500-horsepower Pratt & Whitney engine, on the perilous flight. By sheer coincidence caused by the weather, the departure took place on May 20, 1932, four years to the day after Lindbergh set off for France.

Another pilot took her plane to Newfoundland, while Amelia slept in the cockpit. Once there, they waited for word from New York. The telegram from Putnam arrived informing Amelia that the weather over the Atlantic was right for an immediate takeoff.

She left at dusk, climbed to 12,000 feet, then settled in for what appeared to be smooth flying all the way across. The early calm was illusory. Soon her plane was buffeted by a storm. Amelia decided to fly over it, but the altimeter had gone, and if she flew too high, the wings might ice. At one point, the plane did ice up, sending Amelia into a spin. With consummate skill she waited until the spinning plane had reached an altitude where the ice would melt, then she pulled the plane out into level flight, while the whitecaps on the waves loomed uncomfortably close below.

By now she had passed the point of no return and had no alternative but to continue on to Europe, through the heavy clouds that engulfed her. Every few minutes she would adjust the Sperry gyroscope to a new bearing and occasionally take a drink from a can of fruit juice. The routine continued throughout the night.

Finally daybreak came and Amelia squinted through the early light for the sight of land. As her anxiety mounted, she suddenly spotted the distant contours of the coast of Ireland. Had the flight been smooth, she would have flown on to Paris, but that was out of the question now. Instead, she found a smooth meadow, set the plane down, cut the switches, and watched an awestruck farmer approach the plane.

"Hello," she said with a wide, relieved grin. "I've come from America."

Denis Keyser rubbed his eyes and contemplated three days' work scattered on top of the desk. Before him lay six books, two of them written by Amelia Earhart herself, a stack of newspaper clippings from the morgue, and three spiral notebooks full of scribbled notes. The tiny bachelor apartment was in worse shape than usual, with clothes strewn about, empty beer cans sitting on the small kitchenette table, and a snappy ten-speed bicycle resting against an overcrowded floor-length bookcase. Although he was blessed with an orderly mind, Denis' sense of organization did not extend to neatness.

In a corner of the desk, a stack of bills stood ominously, begging for attention. It was late in the month and Denis wondered how many checks he could kite until payday. He riffled through the stack of multicolored envelopes, yellow for Bloomingdale's, buff for the phone company, blue for Con Ed, and assorted shades for the others, and found a handwritten letter, the first non-computer-addressed communication he had received in months. Denis instantly recognized his mother's handwriting.

He sighed as he began to read the letter, knowing that in his family bad news came by mail. Good news prompted phone calls. The letter stated the case simply enough. Father had lost another job; he had become depressed about their financial predicament but was too proud to ask.

Denis put the letter down and addressed an envelope to his old home in the Bronx. He wrote a short note, made out a check for fifty dollars, enclosed them, and sealed the envelope. After he made the entry, his check register showed a balance of eighteen dollars. By mental telepathy he informed Bloomingdale's that the store would have to get along for another month without his payment. He would survive the remaining days until payday on "plastic," thanks to Master Charge and other establishments who still trusted in his future. "Sacha, dear, I hope you're not expecting a regal dinner tonight," Denis said aloud to himself.

Lumumba, Denis' three-year-old golden retriever, yapped twice at the sound of the word "dinner."

"Jesus, I'm sorry, old buddy," Denis said. "I almost forgot to feed you."

Denis opened a box of Gainesburgers and poured some in a bowl. "I hope you don't mind if we share next week. This stuff starts to smell good when I'm broke."

Lumumba wagged up a storm and began chomping at his dinner.

The doorbell rang. Denis unfastened two bolts and opened up to find Sacha struggling with a large white pizza box and a bottle of rosé. He helped her with the pizza and found her cheek for a gentle kiss. "Hey, hon. You didn't have to. I thought we'd go out," he said as sincerely as he could.

"Don't be a silly goose. It's the end of the month and you're probably broke. I just got paid for a photo job, so

33

let's eat in." Sacha wore a scarf tied tightly around her head. She quickly removed it and tossed it on the bed. Then she took off the brown cardigan, revealing a pink silk blouse, no bra, tucked into the long peasant skirt. "Besides"—she smiled, her eyes sparkling—"I've got ulterior motives."

"You're fantastic," Denis said as he held her and squeezed her tightly. He loved her dearly and had no doubt that this was the woman he would like to have for his wife, just as soon as he could save a few dollars to make it happen.

"How are your parents?" Sacha asked, spotting the handwritten note on the desk.

"Not so good," Denis replied. He reached for two plates in the kitchen cupboard. "Dad lost another job, so I'll have to help out a bit."

"Just what your budget needed, eh?" She took the plates from Denis and put them on the table.

"What else can I do, Sacha?" Denis raised his arms slightly in a gesture of exasperation. "My mom worked eight years waiting on tables to help send my brother and me to college, and look what she got: an unemployed teacher and an underpaid newsman. Shit, I feel I owe them something."

"You know I'll help if I can. . . ."

Denis sighed. "Thanks, sweetheart. But that's not the answer. If I'd only been three inches taller, I'd be making a fortune in the NBA."

Sacha shook her head. "That's a lot of shit, Denis. You always wanted to be a newspaperman, not a basketball player. Your mother told me that." She let slip a mischievous grin. "Besides, I understand you're a better writer."

Denis crumpled a napkin and took aim at Sacha. She raised her hands to parry the projectile. Instead, Denis took a jump shot across the room and watched the wad sink into the wastebasket. "One thousand four hundred and sixty-two," he said calmly.

Denis found his solitary candle and prepared to set the rickety wooden table while Sacha made a heroic attempt to put some order into the place, discarding beer cans, picking up clothes, trying unsuccessfully to find a better place for the bicycle. "Don't ever ask me to live with you, slob," she said half-jokingly.

They ate the pizza while it was still warm, and soon Sacha was brimming with questions about Amelia Earhart. She had seen the news report on television and wondered if it was really possible that the famous woman air pioneer was still alive.

"It's possible, all right," Denis said, speaking to her across the table by the light of the flickering candle. "She'd be in her late seventies by now. The Australian woman fits the description. I understand her looks are close enough."

"Did you finish your research?"

"I don't know if it's finished, but I do know a hell of a lot more about Amelia Earhart than I did before. She was an impressive lady."

Denis recounted to Sacha some of the details and anecdotes about Amelia Earhart that he had uncovered during his brief but intensive research effort. He spoke wistfully of her single-minded determination to be a pilot, of the many stumbling blocks that had been thrown her way, including her father's alcoholism, her parents' financial and marital difficulties, and, of course, the fact that she was a woman and an early feminist. As he spoke of her, Sacha could feel the admiration in his voice and suddenly she felt touched with envy.

"Our backgrounds were quite similar, you know," Denis added, pouring another glass of wine. "Her parents were educated but poor, her father suffered terribly from a problem with the bottle, and she had to fight to get what she wanted. Quite a woman."

"Well, it might have been easier in those days, you know," Sacha commented. "Most women didn't do anything except warm bottles. She didn't have much competition."

"Right you are, honey. And she could have easily rested on her false laurels after becoming the first woman to fly the Atlantic. But she didn't."

Instead, Denis related, Amelia became frustrated at having been a mere passenger on the flight—as useless, as she had put it, "as a sack of potatoes." That was when she decided to make a solo flight across the Atlantic, to prove that she was the equal, as a pilot, of any man.

Sacha fought off the pangs of jealousy while Denis spoke of Earhart in admiring tones, but the pout on her face gave her away. "Denis, maybe you need a woman like that. Some kind of amazon you can respect!"

"Whoa!" objected Denis, raising his hand. "First of all, I love you, and I couldn't do that if I didn't respect you. You happen to earn my respect in lots of ways. You don't need a pilot's license for that."

Denis rose from his chair and kissed her softly. He knew that Sacha had difficulty articulating her hurt feelings, so that verbal arguments invariably frustrated her. He had learned long ago to avoid them.

Soon they were kissing passionately and Denis began to unbutton her blouse. They glided over to the bed and made love with tenderness. In the afterglow, any problems that may have existed before seemed far away. Sacha lit a cigarette and sat up naked in the bed, her silky skin reflecting the candle's glow from across the room. Denis admired her body with a deep sense of satisfaction, ever grateful that she loved him as much as he loved her.

"What's next?" Sacha asked.

"Honey, I don't know if I'll be able to again. . . ."

Sacha laughed. "No, silly. I meant about the story."

Denis smiled broadly and sat up, folding his arms around his knees. "The news dispatch mentioned a Project Sherman. Supposedly the Earhart woman said something about it. I couldn't find anything by that name in the morgue except for some unrelated material on the Sherman tank. I've got a couple of people to talk to, though."

"Not in Australia, I hope."

"No, my editor nixed that. One possible source is an Army officer. His name's Cerilla. Every time in the past few years that some old lady claims to be Amelia Earhart—

and there have been quite a few cases of that—this guy seems to be on the scene snooping around. I found his name in some of the press reports, although he never would comment on why he was there."

"Were you able to locate him?"

"Yeah, at the Pentagon. I made an appointment for next week. I can't say that Cerilla sounded overjoyed to hear from me, but at least he didn't refuse."

"Who's the other person you want to talk to?"

"A college professor. Peter Sloan. He's in Washington, too. Teaches at Georgetown. I ran across his name several times. They say he's an expert on Amelia Earhart and the area in the Pacific where she went down."

Sacha sat quietly for a moment, her attention drifting away.

"What are you thinking?" Denis asked.

"Strange, isn't it?" she commented, drawing a long puff on her cigarette. "They never found her or her plane, did they?"

"Nope. It's one of the great mysteries of the century, and that's a good enough reason to do this story. The Sherman business intrigues me, too. Anyway, Earhart's plane vanished off Howland Island, in the South Pacific, back in 1937, and we don't know any more about it today than we knew then."

"I gotta go," Sacha said. "Early job tomorrow." As she rose from the bed, Denis sat quietly, admiring for the hundredth time Sacha's trim, nude body. Soon they were both dressed and Sacha was at the door.

"How long will you be in Washington?" she asked.

"Just a day. I'm going to try to see both Cerilla and Sloan on Tuesday. I've still got some more checking to do in the morgue. That'll account for most of my weekend."

"I'll come in on Tuesday and feed Lumumba."

"Thanks, darling." He kissed her and watched her walk down the dimly lit hallway. "And stay away from those lecherous Madison Avenue types."

chapter
4

Amelia Earhart and her publisher husband, George Putnam, enjoyed many of the perquisites of celebrity, including invitations to the White House, which later led to a genuine friendship between the Putnams and the Roosevelts.

One evening, while dining at the White House, Amelia waxed enthusiastic over the exhilaration of night flying to Eleanor Roosevelt, and the spectacular sight of the stars when viewed from an airplane. The First Lady was visibly fascinated, so Amelia took the story to a natural conclusion: she invited Mrs. Roosevelt for a night flight that very evening. Without informing either of their husbands, the two women, dressed in evening gowns, sped off to National Airport, where Eastern Airlines cheerfully agreed to the loan of a plane. With the First Lady in the copilot's seat, the two women set off on a flight over Washington and the surrounding suburbs.

Soon after the experience, Eleanor Roosevelt decided that she too would like to become a pilot, and she went so far as to take the required medical examination (from a doctor friend of Amelia's), and acquired a student flying permit.

Then came the time to break the news to FDR. Upon

learning of the scheme, the President would not even consider it, and the idea was firmly put to rest.

Denis worked carefully. He rubbed the spots gently with alcohol, hoping the stains would disappear. It was his only suit, a blue striped worsted, appropriate enough for a spring day.

This time, the spots came off and even Lumumba seemed pleased, wagging his tail and slobbering about his master's face. "Move, Lumumba!" Denis scolded as he pushed the animal away. "That damn train leaves in an hour and I've got to look my Establishment best. Sacha'll be over to feed you. You like that, don't you?" Lumumba was now back over on Denis, who put the suit down and sparred playfully with the dog. "You horny devil. Now, you behave while I'm gone, you hear?"

The Metroliner eased out of Pennsylvania Station at 7:30 A.M., right on time. Denis appropriated two seats in the half-filled car and spread himself out. To his fellow travelers the young man might have been an attorney for a Wall Street law firm, on his way to Washington to plead his client's case before the SEC. His blue suit was complemented by a conservative striped tie and blue shirt. If only Latelle could see him now.

Denis opened the attaché case his mother had given him on his graduation from college. It had one of those faggy green-and-red stripes down the middle, and Denis hated it. But he used it anyway, knowing that its equally fancy price probably cost his mother a week's wages. From inside the case he pulled out a book on Amelia Earhart. On the cover, a likeness of Amelia stared at him. He stared back, sensing that he wanted to know this woman. A thousand questions popped into his mind, begging to be answered. Had she really died on her last flight? Was it true that she had been part of a secret government mission to spy on the Japanese? Was Mrs. Emily Stenemond, of Sydney, Australia, really Amelia Earhart?

On arrival in the District, Denis allowed enough time to take the bus to Georgetown, thereby saving a few dollars on expenses. This trip was being financed out of his own pocket. Besides, Denis didn't trust any taxis without meters. As the bus wended its way through downtown Washington, Denis speculated about what life in New York would be like with meterless cabs like those in Washington. "Let's see, ma'am, that's three zones from Thirty-fourth Street to the Plaza, plus the zone we nicked crossing Fifty-seventh Street. Let's call it twelve-fifty with the tip."

The bus stopped at Thirty-seventh and O streets and Denis gazed at the imposing Gothic buildings on the Georgetown campus. It's like Chartres right in the city, he thought. A helpful gate guard directed him to the administration office building and from there he received further directions to Dr. Peter Sloan's office in the Healy Building.

Denis entered the small office to find Peter Sloan, associate professor of Far East history, peering at him over his wire-rimmed glasses. A buxom young coed stood before the cluttered desk. She wore an out-of-fashion miniskirt which highlighted her very-much-in-fashion legs.

"Oh, I'm sorry," Denis apologized. "I didn't realize you were busy."

"Mr. Keyser?" Sloan guessed. "No, it's all right. We were just finishing." Sloan wore a light cord suit which contrasted markedly with his darkish skin and smooth black hair. "I'll see you in class tomorrow morning, Julie."

The pert blond gave Denis a hint of a cold look when she passed him on the way out. Denis figured he had interrupted something more interesting than a student-faculty conference.

Sloan rose and this time greeted Denis affably, offering him the only other chair, which was already occupied by a small stack of books. "Oh, they belong to that student," Sloan said apologetically. "She always forgets something."

Without making it obvious, Denis looked intently at the professor, attempting to take the measure of the man. He guessed that Sloan was about forty, with some Latin or southern European forebears to account for the dark hair and skin.

After a few minutes of idle chitchat covering everything from the Washington weather to teaching under Jesuit supervision, both men were prepared to address the purpose of the meeting. Denis stated simply enough that he had been assigned to follow the Earhart reincarnation and in the course of his research so far, he had learned that Dr. Sloan had written several articles about Amelia Earhart's disappearance. In one of the articles, Sloan had suggested that the aviatrix had agreed to a secret mission to determine whether or not the Japanese, in violation of their League of Nations mandate, had been fortifying and arming the Micronesian islands, including the Mariana, Caroline, and Marshall island groups, formerly administered by Germany.

"Yes . . ." Sloan confirmed pensively. "But it is not quite that simple." The professor paused for a moment, then continued. "You see, Denis—may I call you Denis?—you have to understand what was happening in this country in 1937 to appreciate the depths of the Earhart mystery. Let me show you something."

He opened a desk drawer and retrieved a large manila file. From it he removed an old front page of a newspaper. Denis recognized the typeface instantly. It was the *Herald Tribune*. "This edition dates back to July 1937," Sloan said. "Look at the headline."

Denis saw the bold letters announcing that Amelia Earhart would take off that day for Howland Island. "Now, look at this story," Sloan continued, pointing to the lower-left-hand corner of the page.

The article was almost a scare piece, warning of the dangers to America of Japanese expansion, currently under way.

Sloan folded the paper in four and put it down. He steepled his hands and spoke. Denis feared that Sloan's History 101/102 was about to convene.

While Denis listened, the professor expounded on the state of U.S.-Japanese relations in 1937. Well into the late thirties, the American government was worried about a possible war with Japan. Roosevelt was indignant about Japan's violation of its mandate in fortifying the Micronesian islands. With strategic control of those islands, the Japanese could use them as forward bases for an eventual attack on Pearl Harbor. Yes, Sloan insisted, even in 1937 people worried about a sneak attack on Pearl Harbor, even though the actual event would not take place for another four years.

This concern had even earlier roots: back in the 1920s Billy Mitchell not only predicted the Japanese attack on Pearl, he boldly suggested it would happen on a Sunday.

Sloan spoke in an enthusiastic voice, quite unlike those of the monotonous lecturers Denis remembered from his own college days. The professor obviously knew his material well, and he made it more interesting by peppering his narrative with relevant anecdotes.

"Now, of course," Sloan continued, "if only we could have gone into the Micronesian islands and actually have proven that the Japanese were fortifying them, the United States would have had a case against Japan. But any attempt to reach those islands, by air or sea, was met with direct hostility. Several airplanes that ventured into the area were simply shot down. You can perhaps see why Miss Earhart's flight offered a tempting opportunity to the President. Here was a world-famous flier who was embarking on a well-publicized around-the-world flight. Were she to lose her way and accidentally fly over the mandated islands— perhaps even photograph them—the Japanese could hardly shoot her down as a spy!"

"I see your point," Denis commented.

Sloan leaned back in his chair and chuckled. "I've got another little story for you. It happens that President and Mrs. Roosevelt were quite friendly with Amelia Earhart and her publisher husband. Most people still don't realize that. One night, after a White House dinner, Amelia even took Eleanor Roosevelt on a secret night flight, just for fun. The fact that Roosevelt and Earhart were friends may have made it easier for the President to ask her to undertake a government mission. Amelia Earhart was, above all, a patriot, and would have been unlikely to turn the President down."

"But does any of that convince you that the woman in Australia could really be Amelia Earhart?" Denis asked.

Sloan nodded. "I can think up at least a dozen ways Earhart could still be alive." He pointed to a bookcase behind him. "See over on the right side of the second shelf? Those are all books about Amelia Earhart. Some of them claim she is still alive somewhere, or at least that she didn't die in the plane crash. But there is no real proof."

While Sloan spoke, Denis scribbled notes in his reporter's pad. Sloan paid no attention. He was used to people taking notes when he spoke. Denis stopped writing momentarily and asked, "What do you make of this Project Sherman business? There was no mention of it in the stuff that I read."

Sloan ventured a thoughtful smile. "That, my friend, is the most interesting part of Mrs. Stenemond's claim. I've come across the name Sherman before. It was about a year ago, while I was doing some research in China."

Sloan explained that one of his sources, an old professor of history in Canton, told him that the United States made a secret loan to China in 1937. It was 100 million dollars in gold, which was loaded onto a U.S. destroyer destined for Shanghai. But the ship never arrived.

"I still don't see the connection with Project Sherman," Denis said, when Sloan had apparently ended his story.

"Perhaps you will, Denis," Sloan rejoined with a twinkle in his eyes, "when I tell you that the name of that destroyer was the USS Sherman."

Denis allowed this last bit of information to sink in. "So there might be some connection between the USS Sherman and Amelia Earhart."

"Quite possibly," Sloan replied. "The timing was right. Amelia's last flight and the disappearance of the Sherman—

if that story is true—occurred in July 1937. Is there enough of a story for you here?"

"It's potentially a great story. But right now it raises more questions than it answers. Besides, I'd hate to run the story of the *Sherman* without some kind of confirmation."

"Well, I've tried every source I know, in academia, and in the government, to get confirmation of the American loan to China. Either no one has heard about it or it is a secret they will not discuss."

"It should be easy enough to confirm the existence of the ship, though," Denis said while he packed his attaché case and prepared to leave. "I've got an appointment at the Pentagon this afternoon. Maybe I'll get lucky and get some kind of confirmation of your *Sherman* story, too."

"I hope you do," Sloan said quite sincerely. "There's a lot at stake, my friend. Perhaps for both of us. I have been gathering information for a new book about Amelia Earhart. The story of this woman, Mrs. Stenemond, plus the *Sherman* episode, would make fascinating material. So I'll appreciate your sharing any findings with me. In fact, why not stay for lunch? We can talk some more."

chapter
5

Courage is the price that Life exacts for
  granting peace.
The soul that knows it not, knows no release
From little things;
Knows not the livid loneliness of fear,
Nor mountain heights where bitter joy can
  hear
The sound of wings.

—Amelia Earhart

The sergeant at the visitor's reception desk confirmed that Denis Keyser had an appointment to see Colonel Stanley Cerilla.

"Please wear this badge at all times while in the Pentagon," the sergeant said in a stiff voice. "You have here a diagram of the building which will direct you to Colonel Cerilla's office."

Denis glanced at the card, oriented himself toward the corridor marked off in bold ink, and set off. A steady stream of pedestrian traffic flowed on both sides of the endless corridor, mostly uniformed men and women whose faces mirrored the gravity of whatever mission propelled them from one office to another. Denis felt slightly self-conscious, not so much because of his civilian dress, which was common enough, but his over-the-ears hairstyle was a rarity among the staunch individuals he passed on his way. When added to a very personal dislike for the military, these impressions made Denis eager to complete his business and get out.

A brown cardboard sign with gold letters confirmed that Denis had found the right door. He knocked and entered, as the sign further suggested, and was greeted by a smiling secretary. Seconds later he was shown into Colonel Cerilla's drab office, where the colonel, clad in a khaki uniform, greeted him from behind his gray metal desk.

The two men shook hands and got right down to business. Denis retrieved his notepad from the attaché case, and sat in a straight chair opposite Colonel Cerilla. He explained that he had been assigned by his newspaper to follow the Amelia Earhart story and had uncovered Cerilla's name during the course of his background research. As usual, Denis tried several tricks to size up Cerilla as an interviewee, and his initial impression was that the colonel would tell him as little as he possibly could. Grudgingly, Cerilla confirmed that he had "routinely" investigated several Amelia Earhart reincarnation stories, only to discover that they were all fakes.

"Have you ever heard of Project Sherman, Colonel?" Denis asked matter-of-factly.

Cerilla tried to conceal his reaction but Denis' skilled eye caught the stiffening. "I read about Project Sherman in the paper. The woman in Australia mentioned it, didn't she?"

"Yes, she did," Denis replied, picking up the tempo to throw Cerilla off, not giving him time to compose his answers. "But had you heard of Project Sherman before that?"

"Uh, I . . . well, I can't really comment on that, Mr. Keyser."

"All right, Colonel. Let me tell you what I know from

unimpeachable sources. Project Sherman refers to a ship, the USS *Sherman*, which was transporting one hundred million dollars of gold to the Chinese back in 1937. The ship, and its cargo, disappeared without a trace."

Cerilla listened stolidly, although Denis could almost see the blood thumping in his temples. "Where in the world did you hear that?" Cerilla asked feebly.

"I can't tell you where I heard it, Colonel. I'd just like to have your comment on the story."

"I have none."

"Would you care to deny it?"

"Mr. Keyser, I have no comment at all."

"In that case, Colonel, I have no further questions. Many thanks for your time." Denis put his notepad back into the case and rose to leave. Cerilla walked around the desk to see him to the door. "Do you plan to do a story on this *Sherman* business?" Cerilla asked tentatively.

"I really can't say," Denis replied coolly. But he noticed the concern in Cerilla's eyes. Denis decided to keep the conversation alive as they moved out. "Say, Colonel, as a man who has obviously studied Amelia Earhart's life story, would you mind telling me what you personally think of her?"

Cerilla didn't answer right away. The two men arrived at the door, and only then did the colonel choose to answer. "I've always admired her courage. Those flights were very risky."

"Do you think she's still alive?"

Cerilla had no intention of fooling with that question. "Good-bye, Mr. Keyser."

When Denis had finally left the office and its adjoining area, Cerilla placed a call to the Secretary of Defense. He got through without delay.

"A reporter's just been here, Mr. Secretary. He knows the story of the *Sherman*, and I'm damned if I can figure out where he got it."

"I don't like the sound of this, Colonel," the Secretary said gravely. "Did you lie to the man?"

"No, Mr. Secretary. But I had to duck all of the direct questions."

"All right. Now we've got to find out who's responsible for this leak. What about security in your department?"

"Mr. Secretary," Cerilla began in a defensive tone, "I've been working with the same group of officers for years. I'll swear that the leak didn't come out of here."

"Well, goddammit, Colonel, who the hell else knew about this!"

Cerilla was stunned at the Secretary's outburst, the first time he had known the man to lose his temper.

After a heavy three seconds' silence, the Secretary continued. "I apologize for my temper, Colonel, but it merely underscores the gravity of the situation we face. I spoke to the President earlier today. He reacted as I had predicted. We do not want that gold falling into anyone else's hands. And, Colonel, I don't want the President embarrassed by our tiny role in a forty-year cover-up."

"I understand, sir."

"You're up for promotion to brigadier general next year, and I'd like to help you get it."

"Thank you, sir." Cerilla understood instantly that the Secretary's support had strings attached.

"Now, you use any legal means at your disposal to plug that leak. And for God's sake, let's find out if that woman is really Amelia Earhart."

Denis dropped two dimes into the pay phone at Washington's National Airport, mumbled something about the price of phone calls in the nation's capital, then dialed Peter Sloan's number.

"Peter? It's Denis Keyser. I'm surprised to find you at the office so late."

"My friend, life in academia is not quite so lethargic as folklore suggests. Are you still in town?"

"For a few minutes anyway. I'm about to catch the seven-o'clock shuttle to New York. Peter, I'm very grateful to you for the *Sherman* story."

"Was the Pentagon visit any help?"

"Yes and no. The good colonel no-commented on everything, but in my business that's often as good as confirmation. After I saw the colonel, I went to the Pentagon archives—the ones that are not classified. I've got at least one bit of hard news for you."

"Yes?"

"There was a USS *Sherman*. A destroyer commissioned in 1934. She was lost in 1937."

"Well done, Denis! Now what do you plan to do?"

"I'm going to take a chance and submit the story of the *Sherman* tonight. Thanks again. I gotta run."

chapter
6

On six separate occasions between 1928 and 1930, George Putnam proposed to Amelia Earhart, and was turned down each time. Amelia had developed misgivings about marriage, due, understandably, to her recollection of her parents' unhappy relationship. She also feared the effects of permanent marital ties on her career.

Soon after his divorce from his third wife, Putnam proposed again to Amelia, and this time, to his surprise and shock, Amelia said yes.

The wedding was as unconventional as its participants. Instead of the traditional bridal gown, Amelia wore an old brown suit and brown lizard shoes. Before the ceremony, Amelia gave the bridegroom a chilling letter spelling out her conditions of marriage.

> . . . In our life together I shall not hold you to any medieval code of faithfulness to me, nor shall I consider myself bound to you similarly. . . .
>
> Please let us not interfere with each other's work or play, nor let the world see private joys or disagreements. . . .
>
> I must exact a cruel promise, and this is that you will let me go in a year if we find no happiness together.
>
> I will try to do my best in every way.

Denis leaned back in his chair and turned the page of the newspaper to find the continuation of his story. A thin smile of satisfaction formed on his face as he read the last paragraph.

> ... Navy records confirm that the USS *Sherman*, a destroyer, was lost while cruising in the South Pacific in July 1937. A leading China expert, who asked not to be identified, said that the gold was destined for Shanghai as part of a U.S.-government loan or grant to China. Officials at the State Department and Pentagon had no comment.

From the corner of his eye Denis saw Latelle charging through the newsroom, a copy of the late-morning edition in his hand. His eyes fixed Denis as he bore down on the young reporter.

"Who the hell approved this story!" Latelle bellowed, pointing to Denis' piece on the *Sherman* and the gold.

Denis stood up, a little shaken by the outburst. "Garrett approved it last night. I submitted it late and you'd already gone—"

"Jesus Christ! Is this what they teach at journalism school?" Latelle slapped the paper with the back of his hand. "Goddammit, Keyser, this isn't a story, it's a fucking rumor! You work for a newspaper, not Rona Barrett's Journal. Are you sure you know the difference?"

"All right, Herb," Denis said defensively. "I knew it was thin, okay. But I believe that story about the gold. My primary source got it straight from China, and then the Pentagon wouldn't comment. Add the fact that the woman who says she's Amelia Earhart talked about Project Sherman, and I think it adds up to a big story. I wanted to be sure we had it first, that's all."

"Enough, enough," Latelle said, exasperated. "You stay on this story, Keyser. And you'd better prove it right or we'll be the laughingstock of New York City."

The view from the eighty-ninth floor of the World Trade Center in New York dazzles the eye and commands respect from all who behold it. Jason Caldwell ambled to the window of the expansive trading room every weekday morning, checked the horizon for clarity and air quality, paid silent tribute to the Statue of Liberty, then proceeded to his desk in the adjoining brokerage office. The routine never varied: Jason brought his cup of Chock Full o' Nuts coffee in a paper bag, read parts of *The New York Times*, the *New York Daily Press*, and the *Wall Street Journal*; then spent a few minutes punching out quotes of a few stocks on the Quotron machine, after which he was ready for work. Habits like these were not acquired overnight. They required years of strict enforcement so that they became second nature, resistant to change, a rut. At fifty-seven, Jason Caldwell did not contemplate changing much of anything, except perhaps his deteriorating financial condition.

His younger colleagues tolerated Jason condescendingly. To them Jason was part of a dying breed of older stockbrokers who had never attended college, knew very little about finance or economics, and got business from a flock of old cronies with whom they had dealt over the years.

The younger brokers sometimes snickered at Jason when he floundered in statistics at the weekly office meeting; and the knowing smiles always followed him when Jason unobtrusively stole down the corridor to the office of Peggy Allenby, a young research analyst with whom, everyone suspected, Jason was having an affair. But why not? He was physically fit, a good-looking man with sandy brown hair and a handsome face, who could easily pass for a man ten years his junior.

"Market open!" one of the brokers shouted. The electronic tape on the wall in front of the brokers' row of desks lit up and began to whir. Now the opening prices flashed by, a rhythmic succession of electronic wizardry.

"GM up a quarter!" someone shouted. "Stocks are higher."

Jason paid no attention to the excitement around him. The truth was that he had little business these days, and few customers to call. Many had moved, some had died, and Jason Caldwell was not inclined, at his age, to start pounding the pavements in search of new ones.

How he had come to hate this job! In the beginning, the thrill of being a stockbroker, outguessing the market every day, picking stocks that others would buy later and send the prices skyrocketing—all of this had enthralled Jason, and in the process he had become a very successful customer's man. But that had been years ago. The disillusion of countless bear markets and the deterioration of his enthusiasm for picking stocks that seemed to do everything but go up had taken its toll and finally replaced his enthusiasm with a cynical skepticism that gradually killed off his business. Clients expect optimism from their brokers. A broker who is not cheerful, not optimistic, not confident about tomorrow's prices, does not get orders. And a broker who does not get orders does not get paid.

Jason removed his jacket and draped it over his chair behind the third desk in the second column of brokers. Normally he kept his coat on, considering it proper and indispensable during the business day. But the fraying of the sleeves on his suits, which he could no longer afford to replace, compelled Jason to remove his coat, against his better instincts, to avoid the embarrassment of so telling a sign of his declining financial situation.

Jason looked around. All of his smart-aleck colleagues were in place, ready to begin calling their customers to inform them of the opening tendency of the market. Instead of the phone, Jason picked up the *Daily Press*, preferring, at least this morning, its lighter style to the more serious content of *The New York Times*. He scanned the headlines—another nursing-home scandal—and thought how much he would like to give up his job. The only joy left in coming to work was the knowledge that he could see Peggy Allenby whenever he wished, under the pretense of checking up on whatever stock she was recommending at that time.

As he perused the second page of the *Press*, Jason came

across the story on the *Sherman* and Amelia Earhart, a headline that instantly evoked painful, hidden memories for him.

He read the story once, quickly, and suddenly his heart beat faster and he gasped for breath. *Can this really be true?*

Jason rubbed his eyes for relief; then, his fingers shaking, he picked up the newspaper and with deliberation reread the article about the *Sherman* and its possible cargo of gold.

When he had finished, he tucked the paper and his coat under his arm and headed straight for the Research Department.

Peggy Allenby was on the phone when Jason marched into her office. He motioned her to hang up, which she did, after mumbling a weak excuse to her caller.

"Jason, what the hell is it?" Peggy's attractive angular face showed a few "over-thirty" wrinkles, but her short brown hair and green eyes added up to a good-looking sum total. She wore a businesslike tailored suit and white blouse.

"Let's go downstairs for a cup of coffee," Jason said.

"I've got a couple of calls to make . . ."

"They can wait. What I've got to tell you can't. C'mon."

They found a secluded booth in the brightly lit coffee shop. There were only a few other people in the place, although in about an hour and a half it would be full. They ordered coffee, and Peggy added an order for an English muffin, cursing her lack of willpower. The coffee arrived in seconds and Jason took a slow sip. "Peggy, what is it that you want most in the world?" he asked solemnly.

"You took me away from the office to ask me that!"

Jason smiled nervously. "The question is both important and relevant. Try to answer."

Peggy looked at him quizzically, wondering what strange card Jason might have up his sleeve. What did she want out of life? *Have you got a couple of days to hear me out?* she thought. She sipped the coffee and decided to tackle the question seriously. "Let's divide the answer into two parts," Peggy said, at her analytical best. "Part one is my romantic future; part two is my financial objective."

"Proceed, my dear."

"You know, Jason, that before I found you, my romantic interests were nothing more than a series of sorry affairs with men my own age. I don't know if it's just this town, but men here—at least the ones I've met—only want one thing: to get laid. They play a kind of a numbers game, you know, like they teach the firm's salesmen. If you solicit fifty accounts, you'll open two or three. Well, men in this town play the same game. If you proposition fifty girls, you'll get lucky two or three times. Honest, that's the way it is. And I'm not playing anymore. I had dropped out until I found you. You're mature, sensitive, and you really care. Besides, my shrink says you're good for me. There, did I say all the right things?" Peggy smiled, drank more coffee, and wondered what the hell had happened to the English muffin.

Jason chuckled. "I've always wondered why your psychologist liked me. Especially since we've never met."

"It has something to do with why I love you and why you're so damned important to me. Do you really want to go into all this now?"

"I do."

"Okay." Peggy downed the last sip of coffee and wished there were more. Where was that damn waitress? "The shrink thinks it's interesting that I am attracted to a man who is old enough to be my father. Well, I was never very close to my father, even though when I was a young girl I desperately wanted to be. Instead, the old man drank himself into oblivion and made every attempt to forget a family that was just a noose around his neck. He died when I was thirteen."

"How do you reconcile sleeping with a man who's a father substitute?"

"Oh, Christ, Jason. It's never that simple. You're a father image, not a father substitute. I love you for lots of reasons."

"Then why don't you want to get married, Peggy?" Jason asked softly.

"I don't know, exactly. Freedom, I guess. I can't see myself bound to anyone permanently. I like it the way it is with us. I love you, I respect you, I need you, and I like to think about it every day. Not take it for granted. So I guess my romantic objective is to wake up every morning wanting you and hoping you'll be there."

"All right, darling." Jason smiled. "Now tell me about your second objective."

"Ah, the financial one. Okay, this one is more simple. I hate poverty. I came into this business under the mistaken idea that I could get rich. What a mistake that was! I make twenty-eight thousand dollars a year picking stocks for others to buy, since I don't have enough money to buy them myself. My financial objective, Jason, although I sense it slipping through my fingers, is to be rich as hell."

Now Jason was positively beaming. "What would you say, Peggy, if I told you that I learned today that both your objectives, as well as all of mine, can be fulfilled?"

"I'd say it was wishful thinking or premature senility."

"Then it's time I told you a few things," Jason said solemnly. "First, did you read the story in the *Press* this morning about a ship called the USS *Sherman?*"

"Sure. I read all the stuff about that Amelia Earhart woman. It's wild. Especially that business in today's paper about the gold."

"I'll get to that. Right now, I want to tell you something about my youth." Jason's attention wavered for an instant as he reached far back in his memory. "Forty years ago, as an eighteen-year-old seaman, I was on board the USS *Sherman* on her last voyage." As he retold the tale, the memories came to life, recreating for Jason the agony of nearly losing his life. He told Peggy of his strolls around the deck, whenever he was off duty as the radio operator's assistant, and as he spoke, his voice seemed like that of a young man spinning a tale. Jason loved the feel of fresh sea air on his face, and the special aroma of the South Pacific. The lilting sound of the sea as it was broken by the bow of the ship, and the gentle swaying of the deck underfoot lifted the spirits of the young sailor and allowed him to put aside the memories of a dreary childhood in northern Pennsylvania.

On this occasion, there had been little for him to do, since the ship's radio had conked out two days earlier. Over and over again the chief radio operator broadcast into a dead microphone, hoping that by some miracle the contraption might start up again.

Jason was on the bridge gazing at the contours of a picturesque tropical island whose lush green hills resembled a prehistoric dinosaur, complete with a sloping back and a small tapered-off head. Suddenly an explosion ripped through the ship. He remembered all the thunderous noise, the screams, debris flying in all directions, the deck giving way, crumbling below. He grabbed a piece of railing that was still attached to the side of the ship. As he clung desperately for his life, water rushed around the listing vessel, carrying furniture, supplies, and human beings in its frantic torrent. Something grabbed Jason's leg. He glanced down and saw another sailor looking up at him in terror, his eyes wide and begging.

It was his closest friend, Tom Greene, with whom Jason had shared countless evenings playing cards, worrying about the future, sharing their darkest secrets. Jason grabbed at him while Tom screamed.

"Hang on to him!" yelled another sailor who was himself trapped under a jagged piece of metal.

Jason held the railing with one hand and clutched his friend Tom with the other. The water rushed by them with torrential velocity, and Jason thought his arm would tear off. If he let go of the railing, he would be swept away with the others. If he held on, he would have to let go of his friend to relieve the excruciating pressure.

"Hang on, dammit!" the other sailor shouted.

"I can't," Jason sobbed. "Tom, I can't!"

And Jason let go.

The young man screamed and was swept away in the deadly torrent. He vanished in a matter of seconds.

"You bastard!" yelled the trapped sailor.

Jason's next memory was of floating on a small piece of wood. Although he ached all over, the moans he heard were not his own, but those of some fellow shipmates floating nearby. The sea was cluttered with debris; the ship had vanished.

In his young life, Jason had never before experienced total despair, and now, as he bobbed on the endless ocean, he felt his physical and mental strength seeping away. The agony of having let go of his friend made Jason hope that he too would die. Suddenly he heard a familiar noise. He strained to look around him in a wide arc. Nothing. Then the young sailor gazed skyward, and there it was! A roaring, gleaming, silver twin-engine Lockheed flying low. Of course! It was Amelia Earhart. Everyone on board the *Sherman* knew about her flight and had hoped to get a glimpse of her near Howland. Jason tried to wave, but his muscles would not respond. Blackness overcame him again, and all was quiet.

The hospital ward in San Francisco was antiseptic white and on either side of him Jason could see a long row of beds exactly like the one to which he was confined. He had no idea how he had come to be there.

His state of consciousness, the readjustment to life, the feeling of gratitude at having escaped the sea, contrasting with the painful memory of Tom Greene, were emotions that had been with Jason for only a few hours when the men from the Pentagon arrived. They flashed ID cards and did not smile. The interrogations lasted at least three hours every day as the men pumped the young sailor for every detail he could recall about the "incident." They kept coming back to the same question, and each time they asked it, their tone became more belligerent. What was the ship's location when it went down? I don't know, Jason replied honestly, for at that point he remembered nothing. But you were on deck. Surely you must have heard something, or noticed something. No. No. No. Leave me alone. Ask the others. None of the other survivors was on deck. You are the only one who could know where the ship went down. No. No. No. Leave me alone. They badgered the eighteen-year-old boy until he broke down and cried.

Peggy had not uttered a word while Jason related his experience. There was an eerie eloquence about the way he spoke.

"I was frightened, Peggy. I didn't know what to do. Between those government men and my nightmares about Tom Greene, I nearly lost my mind." Jason paused at the mention of his friend. "I guess that's one of the reasons I never married. I felt jinxed by close attachments. The only close friend I ever had died because of me. You know, Peggy, you're not just my only love, you're my only friend."

"Since you were eighteen?"

"Yes . . . well, almost. There was a brief romance when I was in the hospital. Her name was Rose Mullen. She was a sweet young nurse, I guess twenty at the time. I suppose you could say she was my first love, but after what had happened, I just couldn't let myself get emotionally involved. Anyway, I got out of the hospital after a four-month stay, got my discharge from the service, and headed to Des Moines, Iowa. I think I went there because that's where the first bus was going. I wanted desperately to get away from anything that had to do with the *Sherman* and the other survivors. A few months later I changed my name from Carnoff to Caldwell, and decided to start my life over again."

Peggy looked puzzled. "But were you still afraid of those Pentagon people? You told them everything you knew."

Jason's eyes sparkled as he spoke. "You see, my dear, shortly after I settled in Des Moines, a very strange thing happened. I went to a movie."

"Yes, that is very strange," Peggy said sarcastically.

Jason ignored the crack. "The movie was a travelogue about the South Pacific, a camera crew visiting islands rarely seen by Western visitors and that sort of thing. There were some islands they couldn't visit because of Japanese restrictions, so some places were photographed from the ship, at a distance. Well, one of the islands looked strangely familiar. It resembled a dinosaur with a long tail and high arched back. I stayed and watched the film again, just to be sure. The announcer identified it as the Pingelap atoll, but to me it was the last thing I saw before the *Sherman* blew up."

Now Peggy let it all sink in, her mind ticking off the points Jason had made. "My God, Jason, you mean you know where the ship is? The ship with a half billion dollars in gold?"

"I know *exactly* where it is, my dear."

"But why haven't you *done* something about it in all these years?"

"Because, my love, until today I didn't have the slightest idea that there was a shipment of gold aboard, that's why. The scuttlebutt on the ship was that we were carrying a valuable cargo to China, but nobody knew what it was. I do now."

"You mean there's an absolute fortune out there, underwater, and you are the only person who knows where it is?"

"That's right, except for one thing. There may be two of us who know where the gold is."

"Who's the other one?" Peggy snapped.

"The woman in Australia. She's the one who mentioned Project Sherman in the first place. If she is really Amelia Earhart, then she knows where the *Sherman* sank because she saw the wreckage from the air."

"I guess that means you've got to hurry."

"It means we have got to hurry, darling. I want you to be my partner. But we still have a major stumbling block before us. A salvage operation will cost a lot of money. I'm not sure how we can go about raising it without tipping our hand."

"How much will we need?"

"I'm not sure. Maybe two hundred fifty thousand dollars to start—and that's just a guess. It's an expensive business."

"I'll say it is. I don't have anywhere near that kind of money. I figure I'm worth about eighteen thousand. I suppose I could contribute that much, but I'd hate to lose it." Peggy took Jason's hand in hers and he squeezed it gently.

"I'm afraid the only cash I can contribute will be the proceeds from the sale of my car. Maybe three thousand. I'm sorry, Peggy, but that's all I have."

"So the question is: how do we get from twenty-one thousand dollars to two hundred fifty thousand in a hurry."

Peggy and Jason sat silently for a while, deep in thought. After a few minutes of glum meditation Jason feared that they would never raise the necessary funds for the salvage operation, and a feeling of despair swept over him.

Peggy suddenly looked up, her face fired with enthusiasm. "I've got it!" she yelled. "It's not your lily-white plan, and it violates half a dozen securities laws, but by God, it'll work. It'll get us the money." Slowly and methodically Peggy explained to Jason her little scheme for turning twenty-one thousand dollars into a quarter million in less than two weeks. When she had finished, Jason felt a gush of relief.

"Darling, you're a genius. It's a fantastic plan. And it will work." Jason picked up the check and they both headed for the cashier.

"Darling . . ." Peggy whispered.

"Yes, my sweet," he replied.

"Don't pay for the English muffin. It never came."

chapter
7

The weeks and months that followed her transatlantic flight brought instant fame to the first woman to complete the then perilous air journey, and celebrity had its rewards. Although the country was in the throes of the Great Depression, Amelia Earhart's personal fortunes were decidedly on the rise. Under the financial guidance of George Putnam, the famous aviatrix signed contract after contract for the endorsement of a wide variety of products. In an era when apples were sold from wooden carts on Wall Street by unemployed brokers, Amelia could count on thousands of dollars in income from the endorsement of cigarettes (which she rarely smoked), women's clothing, and a complete line of Amelia Earhart luggage. It all seemed like such an easy way to make money, allowing one's name to be displayed on billboards or identified with some product. But on one occasion Amelia drew the line. George Putnam had signed an endorsement contract for a children's hat with the Earhart signature sewn into the brim. When Amelia saw the finished product, she rejected it outright, considering it shoddily made. Despite Putnam's protests, she stood firm, forcing him to cancel a lucrative contract *at a considerable loss. No matter. There was ample income from the other sources to begin accumulating funds for Amelia's future daring exploits.*

(AP) ** 1440 ** The Associated Press has learned that Emily Stenemond, who claims under hypnosis to be Amelia Earhart, has accepted an invitation by the Stanford Medical Institute to be examined by a team of doctors there. Mrs. Stenemond will also be questioned on various aspects of Amelia Earhart's life, and will undergo physical and psychological examinations to establish whether or not she is the famous aviatrix. Dr. Hans Gruber, director of the Munich Institute of Psychology, will take part in the examination. Although no dates for Mrs. Stenemond's visit have been announced, her arrival in San Francisco is expected sometime next week.

-o-

Denis Keyser grinned from ear to ear as he sauntered back to his desk. His ebullient mood was quickly noticed by several colleagues, who offered various theories to account for Denis' condition. A raise, no doubt. Perhaps he just punched Latelle one in the nose? A popular theory, that one, but more the result of wishful thinking than of thoughtful analysis. Denis stood at his desk, waved to one and all, then picked up his phone to call Sacha.

"Some good news for a change," he said cheerily.

"Please tell me in a hurry, Denis," Sacha whispered nervously, "I'm in the middle of a session with a cranky photographer."

"Hey, what kind of session is that?"

"Knock it off, Denis. I'm modeling coats."

"Only kidding," Denis said, relieved. "Listen, Latelle just told me to go to San Francisco to cover Amelia's examination. He wants me to try to get confirmation of my *Sherman* story so the *Press* will be off the hook. Apparently there was a lot of flak about it."

"I hope you won't be gone long."

63

"Maybe a week. But I want you to come with me. If we can just raise the airfare for your ticket my per diem will cover the rest."

"San Francisco? God, Denis, I don't know if I can. . . ."

"Bullshit. Of course you can. Let's talk about it tonight."

Sacha let out a girlish laugh. "Okay, sport. See you at your place at seven."

Colonel Stanley Cerilla tucked another file into his leather case and rummaged around his desk, looking for needed items he might otherwise forget. An eerie silence hung over the office. The secretaries and staff had departed long ago and the office area remained dimly lit in the absence of its daytime occupants.

As he prepared to close the case, Cerilla reached for the silver-framed photograph. He smiled warmly at the pretty young face, and realized how silly it might seem for a forty-eight-year-old man to carry about a photograph of a woman in her mid-twenties. But how was anyone to know that his wife had died at the age of twenty-four, less than a year after their marriage? In fact, if he were to stand at just the right angle and look through his office window, Cerilla would see the exact spot where the accident had occurred. Perhaps for that reason, Colonel Cerilla never looked out of his window.

He put the framed picture in his case and snapped it shut. Then Cerilla wrote out a note to his secretary.

Letty:
I'll be at the Holiday Inn at Fisherman's Wharf in San Francisco. If any newsmen call, do not inform them of my whereabouts.

Please do two things in my absence: Catch up on filing, and take long lunch hours.

Best
S.C.

Jason Caldwell entered Peggy Allenby's office and quietly closed the door behind him. He checked his watch. 9:30 A.M. Peggy rose and kissed him on the cheek and they both sat on the small sofa along the wall.

"Today's the day, Jason," Peggy said with a tinge of drama in her voice.

"I know," Jason replied solemnly. "Have you decided what stock we'll use?"

"Yes. Devonshire Stores. First thing on Monday, I'm going to put out a glowing recommendation on that stock. It's something I was going to do anyway. It's the most undervalued department-store chain in the business, and their new catalog division is racking up profits you wouldn't believe. I expect every one of our fourteen hundred and fifty brokers to be recommending it to his clients next week."

"All right, then. That gives me three days to accumulate the options. I guess that'll be enough time. I'll buy the out-of-the-money options, as we agreed."

Options were the latest Wall Street phenomenon, allowing speculators, in effect, to bet on a stock's future price. An option on a stock, like an option to buy a house or anything else, gave the option holder the right to buy the stock at a fixed price over a set period of time. If the investor guessed right and the stock went up, the payoff could be very big.

"I checked this morning," Peggy said. "The best ones for our purpose are the October twenties." She leaned forward and glanced at the door. "Jason, make sure no one is nearby."

Jason rose, opened the door and poked his head out, then closed the door again. "All clear."

Peggy returned to her desk and unlocked a drawer. She removed a stack of traveler's checks, some from American Express, others from various banks that offered that service. They were all blank.

She returned to the sofa and handed the checks to Jason. "Now, sign any name you'd like on the top line. It doesn't matter what the name is as long as you sign the same name on the bottom when you cash them."

"Terrific! I'll use at least five different banks to get the cashier's checks. That will take some time, which is short, with only three working days to open the brokerage accounts." Jason sighed again. "Do you think this will work, Peggy?"

"Oh, it'll work. I'm just worried about someone finding out what we're doing." Peggy fumbled for a cigarette and lit it nervously.

"We know the risks..."

"Christ, Jason! If the SEC finds out about this, I will go directly to jail without passing Go and you'll end up selling apples in front of the Stock Exchange. What we're doing is a criminal offense."

"We're not the first ones. A lot of people fool around with inside information. It happens all the time. In fact, hardly a week goes by without one of the salesmen out there getting excited because a corporate buddy leaked an earnings report to him."

"Well, bully for them. I happen to know a guy in the Research Department at BJ&D who's under indictment for buying stock in his mother's account just before he put out a buy recommendation. Compared to what we're doing, that guy looks like an altar boy."

"Do you want to call it off?" Jason asked.

Peggy looked up at him and as she spoke, the edge left her voice. "No," she murmured. "There's too much at stake." She took a last drag from the cigarette and pounded it out in the ashtray. "You'd better get going."

Thirty minutes after leaving Peggy's office, Jason stood in a serpentine queue inappropriately named the "fast line" at the Chemical Bank branch at Sixtieth and Madison. When his turn finally came, he produced $2500 in traveler's checks on which he had signed the name of Jack Whitemore in the upper-left-hand corner. Then, in the presence of the teller, he signed the same name on the lower line

66

and handed the checks to the woman. The teller verified in a glance that the two signatures were identical.

"Would you like that in cash, sir?" she asked politely.

"No, ma'am. I'd like a cashier's check."

"In your name?"

"No. I want it made out to Mr. Chad Nimitz, if you please. I'll spell that for you." And Jason did.

"Thank you, sir. Won't take a minute."

In fact, the procedure took nearly ten minutes, but Jason didn't mind. He would repeat the operation, using different names and varying amounts, at Manufacturers Hanover, Citibank, Irving Trust, and Chase, and he hoped they would all be this efficient.

At 1:35 P.M. Jason emerged from the Chase branch at Park Avenue and Sixtieth Street, with cashier's check number five securely tucked in his inside jacket pocket. He now had in his possession twenty-one thousand dollars in cashier's checks, made out to five fictitious individuals. Phase one of his part of the scheme was over.

Jason checked his watch. There was enough time left to open perhaps two brokerage accounts today, part two of his assigned duties. He knew that this part would be a lot trickier, and he approached the task with trepidation. But onward and upward, he thought, as he made his way to target firm number one.

The large brokerage firm's corner office on Park Avenue conveniently displayed the names of all the brokers who worked there on the front door. Jason picked the last name on the list, figuring it would belong to the newest broker; then he walked in and asked for him. As he had guessed, Mr. Carl Deutsch was very young, probably recently out of the training program, and, as Jason knew only too well, hungry.

Jason introduced himself as a retired merchant who wanted to speculate in the market for fun. He used the name of Chad Nimitz, considering it quite appropriate that the surname was steeped in the highest tradition of American naval history. Jason told the young broker that he had been recommended to him by a mutual friend who preferred that his name not be used.

Carl Deutsch smiled a lot and spoke at some length about the market, eagerly displaying his newfound wisdom. Jason listened patiently and occasionally smiled back.

"You understand, Mr. Nimitz, that there are a few questions I'll have to ask you before we open the account."

Jason nodded, knowing by heart all of the requirements of the New York Stock Exchange for opening customer accounts, requirements which Jason would skillfully steer around in doing business with this eager young broker.

Deutsch asked questions about Mr. Nimitz's employment. None, of course, since he was retired. His net worth? Over a half million. Other securities? Yes, in safekeeping in a bank in Florida. Credit references? Jason gave Morgan Guaranty Trust, since it was the most prestigious commercial bank in New York, as well as the most discreet. Then Jason handed the young man the certified check for $2500 made out to Chad Nimitz. Now, seated by the broker at his desk, Jason endorsed the check by signing Nimitz's name. He then signed the broker's New Account form, plus another form required by the Chicago Board of Options Exchange. Minutes later the account was routinely approved by the office manager, who gazed upon the certified check with a feeling of relief.

"For my first transaction," Jason announced to Carl Deutsch, "I'd like to take a flier in some options. Specifically, I want to buy some options on Devonshire Stores."

"Right, sir," Deutsch replied dutifully, and picked up a book to look up the symbols so he could punch them out on his electronic quote machine. Jason knew all of the symbols by heart, but he waited patiently until the younger broker had looked them up and pressed the buttons on the machine. Now a full display of all the available options on Devonshire Stores glowed on the screen before them.

Devonshire Stores was currently selling at seventeen dollars a share. Jason saw on the electronic display screen that the three-month options to buy Devonshire at twenty dollars a share were selling for forty cents each.

"I'd like to buy some of those," Jason announced, pointing.

"But, sir," Deutsch protested, "I should explain that although those options are only forty cents each, they can only be worth more if Devonshire climbs to over twenty dollars a share. You see, the stock is only at seventeen now, so an option to buy it at twenty isn't worth anything unless the price goes up to over twenty. Do you follow me?"

Jason smiled congenially. "Yes, Carl, I understand what you're saying, but I'm a speculator, remember? I want to gamble a little." Jason allowed the smile to fade from his face. "It's the only excitement in my life since my wife died."

Both men paid a silent tribute to the late Mrs. Nimitz.

"Well, I guess it's okay as long as you understand the risk..." Deutsch said tentatively. "Of course, if the stock went up a lot, you could really make a bundle."

"I know."

"In fact, let's see..." Deutsch continued, taking an optimistic point of view for a change. "If Devonshire went up to, say, twenty-three before your options expire, then your options would be worth at least three dollars, since they entitle you to buy the stock at twenty. On a forty-cent investment, that's one hell of a profit."

"About seven hundred and fifty percent, I figure."

"Yeah, that's the great thing about options," Deutsch said. "But..."

"But what?" Jason asked.

"Well, to be perfectly candid, in my experience as a broker," Deutsch said solemnly, even though his professional experience could be counted in weeks, "most people who play around in options lose their shirts."

It was nearly four o'clock now, and Jason walked at a fast clip down Park Avenue, seeking out another stock-brokerage firm on whom to shower some business. He hoped that the second target would be as easy as the first.

The sign in the window proclaimed the "Stock of the Month," and Jason smiled. Hail to target number two, he thought, as he pushed the glass door open.

"I'd prefer to do business with a younger broker," Jason told the receptionist. "They seem to have more time. . . ."

Jerry Devine was young, all right, two months out of the training program and full of confidence. Was I like that? Jason wondered, as he recalled the countless bear markets he had endured in his own career as a stockbroker. How could any of these young men approach the market with anything but timidity and respect?

"My name is Charlie Forrestal," Jason said, extending his hand to the young man, "and I'd like to open an options account. . . ."

Jason went straight to Peggy's office on Monday morning, bypassing his own desk and forsaking his coffee-and-newspaper ritual.

"It's done," he announced.

"You opened all the accounts?" Peggy asked. She wore a skirt and turtleneck sweater, in contrasting shades of brown.

"I opened five. I had trouble only once. At Merrill Lynch. They wouldn't take my account until they checked me out, so I left in a huff. The other brokers were hungrier, and, therefore, easier. And I know how they feel!" Jason chuckled. "Anyway, there are now accounts all over town memorializing the names of Nimitz, Halsey, Rickover, and Forrestal, and even Doenitz, which I thought was rather sporting on my part."

"How many options did you buy, Jason?" Peggy asked impatiently.

"A total of five hundred. That gives us options to buy fifty thousand shares of Devonshire Stores at twenty for the next three months, since each call option is good for one hundred shares. By the way, I never paid more than forty cents a share for the calls. The total outlay comes to a bit less than the twenty-one thousand dollars. And needless to say, my dear, if Devonshire doesn't go over twenty, those calls will be worthless and we've lost the entire twenty-one thousand."

"Don't worry about it," Peggy said crisply. "My rave recommendation on Devonshire Stores went out over the wire system this morning. I'll issue follow-up recommendations every day to keep the interest alive. When the stock hits nineteen, it will break out on the charts and send the technical analysts into ecstasy."

"And by then the options should be moving up nicely."

"The big move will come after those widely followed technical analysts issue *their* recommendations. Then the speculators will look for the stock to go up into the high twenties, so the options to buy the stock at twenty are going to be very popular."

Technical analysts, or chartists, attempted to predict future stock-price action based on a stock's previous performance, as displayed on a variety of different charts. Invariably, when a stock sold at a new, record-high price, alarms went off and lights flashed in the "War Rooms" of the technical analysts. A new high often meant that the stock had "broken out" of its old trading pattern and its price would probably climb higher. Technical analysts often issued strong "buy" recommendations when a "breakout" occurred.

"It's almost ten o'clock," Jason said. "I've got to get back to my desk before the opening."

Peggy smiled. "You might want to recommend some Devonshire to your clients, too."

Jason rose to leave. "How long shall we keep the options?"

"I figure they'll start moving up today if the stock opens strong. A lot of speculators are going to play this recommendation by buying the options on the stock rather than the stock itself. But if the stock gets up to twenty-five, which could happen in just a few weeks, those options to buy

Devonshire at twenty will have to be worth at least five dollars each. On fifty thousand shares, my dear Jason, that should yield us a return of—"

"Two hundred and fifty thousand dollars," Jason interrupted. "The magic number."

"Market open!" shouted a broker. The electronic tape began flashing numbers in rapid succession across the long narrow strip.

"Hey, Jason," called Bill Connelly, who occupied the desk in front of him. "Did you see that recommendation your friend Peggy put out this morning? Devonshire Stores. Looks like a rocket. We're all buying some."

"Yes, it does look interesting," Jason agreed.

From two desks away, another broker who was listening in yelled out: "Are there any options available on Devonshire?"

"Yeah," Connelly replied. "Octobers, Januaries, and Aprils. Fifteens and twenties. The October twenties look interesting as a spec. They closed at forty cents but you'll never get them at that price today."

A couple of the brokers nodded in agreement. Jason said nothing.

"Have they opened Devonshire yet?" someone shouted.

"I just had the Trading Department on the phone. There's an influx of orders. The specialist hopes to get it opened in a couple of minutes."

A broker pointed up at the electronic tape. "Hey, there it is: DVS opened at 18½, up 1½ on 120,000 shares!"

The brokers cheered at the news, and the hooting and yelling and carrying on went on for several minutes. Jason remained calm, reading the newspaper as he always did. But his heart beat faster.

"Did those options open yet?"

"All DVS options have opened, and, wow! They're all up. The October twenties opened at a dollar. That's the quickest double you'll ever see!"

Now Jason felt his excitement mounting. The twenty-one thousand dollars he had invested in the past few days was worth fifty thousand dollars this morning, and this was just the beginning. As he watched the flickering numbers flash by on the tape, his mind was lulled into a brief trance. He envisioned himself with Peggy on a salvage ship; the air caressed his face and invigorated his lungs. Beneath them lay a treasure worth a half billion dollars.

chapter
8

Mr. Earhart's walk seemed brisker than usual as he approached the large frame house in St. Paul. His freckled, slightly boyish-looking daughter, Amelia, greeted him enthusiastically at the door.

"There's been a train wreck upstate," he said. "I've been asked to help settle the claims."

While her father was packing, Amelia and her mother prayed that this God-sent assignment might provide Edwin Earhart with a chance to leave his humiliating job as a railroad clerk, and help him break the liquor habit that had brought him so low. A short while later, Amelia went to her father's room to help him pack, carefully avoiding any chiding or lecturing references to his drinking. Deep in his suitcase, Amelia found the bottle. She repaired to the kitchen, and as she poured the brown liquid down the drain, her father stormed into the room, his arm raised.

"Father!" the teenage girl cried. "Don't!"

Amelia's mother grabbed Edwin Earhart's arm. Realizing what he had almost done, Earhart apologized, then stole away to his room, unable to conceal the muffled sobs that voiced his shame.

The American Airlines 747 roared down the bumpy runway at Kennedy Airport and lifted off into the clear afternoon sky. As soon as the seat-belt sign went off, Peggy motioned to Jason, pointing her forefinger upward. "How about a drink upstairs?"

"Lovely idea," Jason replied, and he followed Peggy up the small circular stairway to the lounge. They settled in two swivel seats that faced each other over a small table and ordered two Bloody Marys from the smiling stewardess.

"Don't you think it's a bit extravagant to travel first class?" Jason asked solicitously.

"I suppose so," Peggy said, "but I love being waited on!" She squeezed his hand. "Besides, we've got to get used to being rich."

The drinks arrived and Peggy and Jason clinked glasses. A spoken toast was unnecessary. They both knew what it would be.

Peggy smiled radiantly. "I'll never forget the look on Marsden's face when we told him we were leaving! I swear, he stood there for a full minute with his mouth wide open."

"Well, technically we've been granted a leave of absence to pursue a personal maritime-related research and financial project."

"What a load of bullshit that is," Peggy said as she downed the rest of her drink and waved for another. "The whole office is gossiping about our leaving together. I think they suspect we're going off to California to finance a porno movie or something."

Peggy's drink arrived and she traded it for the empty glass.

"Take it easy on those, sweetheart," Jason cautioned. "It's a long flight."

"Jason," Peggy said, her voice growing louder, "stop acting like a father. Don't you understand? I feel liberated! Free! Out from under that crummy job! This is what life is all about."

Outside the window, scattered fluffy clouds hung over the green terrain dotted with farmhouses and an occasional town. The West was yet to come.

"Did you close all of the brokerage accounts?" Peggy asked.

"Every one. Our profits netted out to $254,516. Those brokers hated to see me go!"

"There'll be an SEC investigation, you know," Peggy said in a somber tone.

"I don't know how they could trace it to us, my sweet. My real name never appeared on anything. Not even the traveler's checks. The brokers are the ones who are going to get their wrists slapped for not obeying the 'Know Your Customer' rule."

Peggy nodded. "Some justice, eh?" she said sarcastically. "By the way, where are we staying?"

Jason reached into the inside pocket of his tweed sport coat and took out a piece of paper. "The Holiday Inn in downtown Long Beach. I've made an appointment for us tomorrow with Soapy Denton, the president of Worldwide Salvage Company."

Peggy slurred her words slightly. "Can they handle this job?"

"From what I've been able to learn, they're the biggest and the best in the business. I researched some of the work these fellows have done, and it's quite spectacular. A few times, they've brought up some sunken cargoes where other companies wouldn't even try. I'm afraid this cargo calls for nothing but the best. It won't be easy."

Peggy looked around the small lounge, hoping to find a stewardess to get her another drink, which she clearly did not need. "Jason," she said, "would you ask Cindy, or Tracy, or Stacy, or Mary Lou, or whatever the fuck her name is, to get me another drink?"

"You don't need another drink," Jason admonished her sternly. He got up and took Peggy's hand. "It's about time for lunch. C'mon, I'll help you glide downstairs."

The Holiday Inn looked like a Holiday Inn, complete with swimming pool, dozens of kids, and an ice machine which Peggy found at once. Pat Roselli, the manager, personally showed them to a poolside room and inquired if it would do. It would do just fine, Jason assured him.

Jason and Peggy made love that night with more passion than they had experienced in years. More recently, their lovemaking had become stale and ritualistic, something one does automatically at night after turning out the lights. This time, though, they refound and relived the thrills of an earlier age, nurtured by the excitement of the impending changes in their lives and fortunes.

They both slept restlessly. Peggy tossed under the covers, dreaming of the fortune that would soon be theirs. Jason woke up in a sweat. He was not dreaming of gold. Instead, he endured one of his frequent nightmares about Tom Greene and the endless moment in time when he let go of his friend's hand.

The following morning they breakfasted in the coffee shop, and while Peggy went back to the room to freshen up, Jason cornered Pat Roselli and asked him for directions to Worldwide Salvage.

"Oh, that's down by the marina," Roselli said as he unfolded a map on the counter. "It's easy to get to."

Within minutes Jason was driving their rented Camaro while Peggy tried to decipher three pages of Roselli's "easy" directions. The air was clear and the sun shone benignly, making it pleasant enough to drive without using the car's air conditioner. Peggy gazed longingly at the palm-tree-lined streets with beautiful Spanish-style houses surrounded by velvet green lawns. "That's the way to live," she sighed.

"And we will, my dear. If you will only get me to our destination."

"Right at the second light."

Worldwide Salvage's headquarters were decidedly not what Jason had expected. A simple sign hung above the door to a wooden frame building which was dwarfed by considerablly more imposing brick structures on either side. Behind the buildings, the marina harbored hundreds of vessels, from small Chris Crafts to bulky, no-nonsense working ships of all descriptions.

Jason and Peggy entered the wooden building and faced a counter a few feet in front of them. A large fan blew air in their faces while a typist behind the counter finished a sentence, then looked up and acknowledged their presence.

"We're here to see Mr. Denton," Jason said.

"Oh, yes. You must be Mr. Caldwell. Come right in."

The woman lifted the top of the counter and allowed Jason and Peggy to pass. Then she knocked tentatively on the only other door and a gruff voice bellowed: "What is it?"

Soapy Denton appeared to be in his early fifties and forty pounds overweight. He wore slacks and a long-sleeved, colorfully printed sport shirt. His unmanageable hair and scruffy complexion spoke of a life on the high seas, exposed to a myriad of elements. Denton sat behind a large desk, chomped on a cigar, and said: "Hi."

"May we sit down?" Jason asked.

"Sure. There's another chair over there in the corner." Denton waved to the area with his cigar.

Once they were seated, Jason introduced himself and Peggy and told Denton why they had come: "I'd like to hire you for a salvage job, Mr. Denton."

"Call me Soapy. You're Jason, right?"

"The job I have in mind is far away from here, in the South Pacific."

"I don't care how far away it is. I do care how far *down* it is. Get me?" Denton puffed on his cigar and sent billows of smoke across the room.

"Could we open the window?" Peggy asked.

"Sure, lady." Denton rose and opened the window behind him. The smoke dissipated, and in the distance, seagulls could be heard.

Denton sat back at his desk. "Okay, lay it on me. Cargo. Depth, location, the works."

"I'll give you part of the information now, Mr. Den—uh, Soapy," Jason said, "and we can discuss the rest after we've made the deal."

"Suit yourself."

"At this point, I will not tell you what the cargo is. The location is near the Mariana Islands in the South Pacific. The depth, I believe, is no more than five hundred feet. The target is a ship."

"You want to bring up a ship?"

"No, just the cargo."

"Five hundred feet ain't no picnic, you know. And you're not even sure of the depth." Denton tapped his fingers on the desk. "Where's the cargo?"

Jason described the ship in vague terms, indicating that the cargo was in a secure hold that might require blasting.

"I don't know," Denton said.

"I beg your pardon?"

"I don't know if I want the job. I'd have to use my biggest ship, the *Princess*, and three full crews of divers, demolition experts, the works. A project like this could take months. I don't know if I want it."

Peggy looked straight into Denton's eyes and leaned forward. "Is it a question of money, Soapy?"

Denton leaned back and took another long puff on his cigar. "Honey, it's *always* a question of money." He grinned and stared at the ceiling for a moment, adding up the bill. "Let's see, I'd need twenty-five of the best people in the business, the best equipment, and for all practical purposes I'd be closing up shop here for a couple of months."

"How much, Soapy?" Peggy asked.

"I hope you two have got a lot of money, because I couldn't take on a job like this for less than four hundred thousand."

Jason and Peggy glanced at one another and both of them saw the look of sheer disappointment in each other's eyes. Finally Jason spoke.

"We can't pay that much, Soapy. We can pay you two hundred and fifty thousand. No more."

"Sorry. Not interested." He smiled when he said it.

Jason and Peggy walked out of the office in a daze, certain that their dreams had been shattered. They walked silently to the car, and Jason said, "Wait here a minute."

He turned and went back into the building, leaving Peggy outside gazing at the marina and the boats, and behind them, the great blue expanse of the Pacific Ocean. Peggy lit a cigarette, leaned against the car, and almost started to cry.

Nearly fifteen minutes later Jason emerged from the building and walked briskly to the car. "Let's go," he said.

They got into the car and Jason drove out onto the street.

"Jason! What happened in there?"

"So far, my sweet, nothing. I took a chance and told our friend Soapy what we were after. I think the five-hundred-million-dollar figure impressed him," Jason added laconically. "Then Soapy went on about how the salvage laws were really not clear and that even if we find the gold there could be a court battle, et cetera, et cetera."

"Left at the next corner. What else did he say?"

"To make a long story short, my dear, I offered Soapy ten percent of the find plus the two hundred and fifty thousand if he would take the job."

"Did he agree?" Peggy asked excitedly.

Jason sighed. "He said he'd think about it. That's all he said."

"Shit."

When they had returned to their room, Peggy grabbed the plastic ice bucket and made a beeline for the ice machine. Jason took the bottle of scotch out of one of the suitcases and poured a healthy dose into the plastic glasses provided by the motel. Peggy was back in a flash. The drinks were mixed, toasts quietly made, and the liquor imbibed with a combined sense of need and urgency. Soon they were on their second drink, sitting on the bed, their spirits partially restored, thanks to the improvised cocktail hour. What will we do? Who knows? Is there anyone else we can hire? Doubt it. Worldwide Salvage was really tops, maybe the only people who could pull it off. Fuck Soapy Denton, the greedy bastard. We've still got two hundred and fifty Gs, which isn't a bad consolation prize. But it's not what we're after. It really isn't. That's not what we're here for.

The phone rang. Jason stared at it for a second, then picked it up. He said hello, and spent the next couple of minutes listening. Peggy looked on, bleary-eyed and anxious.

Soon Jason replaced the receiver and looked at Peggy. Now a wide ear-to-ear grin spread over his face as he bellowed: "The greedy bastard agreed to do it!"

chapter
9

On March 17, 1937, Amelia Earhart and her crew, consisting of Captain Harvey Manning, Fred Noonan, and Paul Mantz, who would ride as far as Honolulu, took off from San Francisco on the beginning of their 'round-the-world flight. Despite the advance publicity for the flight itself, the departure time had remained a secret. One newspaper reporter who did learn of Earhart's plans rented a small plane and circled San Francisco Bay waiting for the famous aviatrix to fly by. His efforts were amply rewarded when he captured a stirring photograph of the Electra flying over the Golden Gate Bridge, a photograph that would be seen by millions in their daily newspapers the following morning, and by generations of others to come.

"Denis, I love it here," Sacha said as she slipped into a tiny yellow bathing suit. Their room at the Hyatt Regency in San Francisco was cheerfully decorated with real—not plastic—furniture and boasted a small semicircular balcony overlooking the pool.

Denis, dressed in his business suit, looked attentively at her while she modeled her new bathing suit for him.

"Like it?" Sacha asked as she completed a full circle.

"I'd like it better if I were going down there with you."

"Don't be such a worrywart, Denis," Sacha chided.

"Well, for Chrissake, it doesn't even cover you up right." Denis lowered his eyes to the bottom half of the suit. "I can see a few hairs popping out."

"You're not supposed to look that close!"

Denis tore his attention away from Sacha and glanced at his watch. "I've got to get down to that Medical Institute." He verified that the reporter's pad was securely tucked into his side pocket, checked to see that he had his pen, then kissed Sacha on the forehead. "See you later, kid. Watch out for guys who stare."

The taxi ride to the Medical Institute consumed the better part of an hour, and on arrival Denis had no doubts that he had found his destination. Outside the wide and stately building, television vans from the three networks, and their attendant cables which formed endless serpentine lines on the ground, signaled the location of a major news story. A row of shirtsleeved policemen stood guard outside, and a small crowd gathered, the kind that hangs around any time a television crew is working. Denis flashed his press credentials for the policeman at the door and was allowed to enter. Another guard directed him to the auditorium.

Inside, a restless crowd of reporters waited impatiently for the hospital spokesman to appear on the floodlit stage. Denis spotted several colleagues from *The New York Times* and New York *Post*, and he recognized the television "celebrity announcers" who were also there. Denis took a seat in the rear of the auditorium as a young man appeared onstage, a piece of paper in his hand, and walked tentatively to the lectern. Appeals for quiet echoed around the room as the young man adjusted the microphone, then his glasses, and began to speak:

"Uh, ladies and gentlemen, I'm afraid I don't have much news for you today. I can confirm that Mrs. Emily Stenemond is here and will be examined, starting tomorrow, by a team of specialists from the Medical Institute as well as a government representative assigned to the case."

From the back of the auditorium a gravelly male voice shouted: "What are their names?"

The young spokesman looked up, played with his glasses again, and said, "Uh, the names of the Medical Institute's participants will be found in the handout over here at the left of the stage."

"How about the government rep?" yelled another reporter.

"I'm sorry, but I don't have that information."

A concert of groans pervaded the large hall, and the spokesman's brow broke out in sweat. "Barring any unforeseen difficulties, we plan a press conference next Thursday at three P.M. at which time we will have a statement on our preliminary findings."

Before he could finish the last sentence, half of the reporters in the auditorium were already on their feet, crowding the aisles to the exit. Denis joined the throng shuffling toward the door. A middle-aged reporter in the group looked around and said sarcastically, "That guy must have worked for the Nixon administration."

As the crowd dissipated through the halls outside the auditorium, Denis recognized a familiar face darting by.

"Colonel Cerilla!" Denis shouted, in pursuit. In two seconds he had caught up with the military officer, who today was clad in civilian clothes.

Cerilla turned around and acknowledged Denis with the faintest nod.

"Well, Colonel, I guess your presence here answers the question about the government representative," Denis said.

"You do a lot of guessing, don't you, Keyser?"

"You don't give me much choice, Colonel. Did you like my story on the *Sherman?*"

"I didn't read it very closely," Cerilla lied.

"Well, Colonel," Denis continued as both men walked along a corridor, Cerilla setting the course, "now all I need to do is figure out the connection between the USS *Sherman* and your interest in Amelia Earhart. Strange, isn't it, that Mrs. Stenemond mentioned Project Sherman? What do you think?"

Cerilla stopped abruptly and gave Denis an icy stare. "I have nothing to say to you, Keyser."

"Sure. 'No comment.' Say, Colonel, when do you think your superiors will take the muzzle off you?"

Cerilla did not acknowledge Denis' barb. He continued to walk, this time alone, down the long white corridor.

Denis unlocked the hotel room door and heard the shower running. He removed his jacket, threw it on the queen-sized bed, then loosened his tie. The shower stopped and a few minutes later the bathroom door opened, revealing Sacha with wet hair and a towel wrapped around her. She saw Denis and was startled: "Why didn't you tell me you were back?"

"You wanted me to announce my presence while you were in the shower?"

"Never mind. I just saw *Psycho* on TV."

"You look better than ever," Denis said as he kissed her on the cheek. Sacha's soft skin glistened with moisture in the aftermath of the shower. She returned the kiss, holding the towel in place with one hand. Then she sat on the bed and ran her fingers through her hair.

"I know why you brought me along on this trip," she said. "You needed a secretary." Sacha leaned on the bed, extending her long, sensuous body in a reach for the notepad beside the telephone. She grasped it with one hand and sat erect. "I've got some messages and a present for you."

Denis plopped in the armchair by the bed and felt the tension leave his body. "Let's start with the present."

"Coming right up." Sacha walked over to the corner of the room, the towel still wrapped around her, although a widening slit at the side provided an erotic glimpse of the entire length of her trim body. She opened the top desk drawer and removed a dusty eight-by-ten wooden frame. "I found it in an antique store around the corner," Sacha said proudly. She handed the picture to Denis, whose curiosity and sexual appetite were now both fully aroused.

"Thanks, hon." Denis took the ornate frame in his hands and looked at the picture under the protective glass cover. It was a stunning black-and-white photograph of a twin-engine aircraft flying over the Golden Gate Bridge. In the lower-right-hand corner, a handwritten inscription read: "To Sam, with love and memories, Amelia."

Denis was moved by the picture. It was as thoughtful a present as he could possibly have wished: a photograph of Amelia Earhart's plane, personally inscribed by her. Based on his own research, Denis guessed that "Sam" was Sam Chapman, Amelia's first beau.

"I love it, darling," Denis said. He put both arms around Sacha. "And I love you. I always will."

Sacha grinned and twitched his nose. "Enough of that, you sex fiend! You've got some phone messages to attend to." Sacha picked up the notepad that she had left on the bed. "Your mother called. By the way, she sounded surprised I was here. Didn't you tell her I was coming with you?"

"Mom still thinks hotels check marriage licenses before they let two people register together. Go on."

"She wants you to call back. Didn't sound too good to me. Money problems, I guess."

Denis sighed. "Anyone else call?"

"Peter Sloan from Washington. Wants you to call before seven."

Denis checked his watch. Three forty-five P.M. That left fifteen minutes to reach Sloan before seven, Washington time. Denis retrieved his attaché case from the closet, frowned ritually at the colorful stripes down the middle, and removed his address book. He dialed Peter Sloan's number direct.

"Denis," Sloan said, after they exchanged greetings, "remember my telling you I was gathering material for a book about Amelia Earhart?"

"Sure," Denis replied.

"Well, one of the big New York publishing houses called me this morning. They're interested in my book proposal but they say it's got to be completed fast to coincide with the new interest in Amelia Earhart."

"That's great news, Peter," Denis said sincerely.

"But I could never finish the book in time if I do it alone. I'd like you to collaborate with me. Listen, it's a perfect match. I know most of the background; you're an investigative reporter working on the Earhart story. We could write a terrific book!"

The suggestion caught Denis by surprise. The idea of writing a book had crossed his mind before, but he had never zeroed in on a topic. Now that Sloan mentioned it, Amelia Earhart and the story of the *Sherman* would be a great subject if they could figure out the connection between the two.

"Denis, are you still there?" said the voice on the telephone.

"Yes, Peter. Sorry. You know, I like the idea. In fact, I like it a lot."

"Fine. We'll split everything fifty-fifty. But they'll only give us four months to do it. Okay? Now, Denis, the first thing we must do is track down any survivors of the *Sherman* sinking. Can you help there?"

Denis thought about it for a moment. "I can't count on Cerilla, that's for sure," he said, thinking out loud. "We're not exactly drinking buddies." Then another thought occurred to him. "Say, I've got a contact who might help. I'll get back to you."

As Denis replaced the phone, Sacha, who had been listening attentively, suddenly bristled and asked: "Your contact wouldn't happen to be Susie Mitchell, would it?"

Susie Mitchell, the military correspondent for one of the largest weekly newsmagazines, had earned a towering reputation in her field, not only for her expertise on virtually all military subjects, including sophisticated weaponry, but also for an uncanny ability to wheedle information out of otherwise granite-faced spokesmen. Moreover, Sacha knew that Denis had once engaged in a brief affair with Susie Mitchell while working on a story involving an Iranian arms deal.

"Yes, it's Susie Mitchell," Denis said in a tone of exasperation, "and I'm going to phone her right now." Denis turned the pages of the address book to the M page.

"I'm sure you still have her home phone number," Sacha said sarcastically.

"Cut it, Sacha. This is too damn important for that kind of shit, okay?"

Sacha did not bother to compose a reply. She sat and watched Denis dial the number in Washington.

"Susie? It's Denis. Denis Keyser," he announced cheerfully. "I'm calling you from San Francisco."

They bantered about for a few minutes, inquired of several mutual friends, then Denis got to the point of the call.

"I need your help with something, Susie," Denis said, while Sacha sat nearby and conjured up variations of Susie's response to that statement.

Denis explained that he was working on the *Sherman* story and needed some information to pursue the research. Had Susie seen his piece in the *Press* on the *Sherman?* Yes, indeed. Intriguing story. Denis wondered if Susie might help him track down the names of any *Sherman* survivors.

"On one condition," Susie said in a businesslike manner.

"Name it."

"I want an exclusive on your story for the newsweeklies. I'm not going to help you if *Time* ends up running it before me."

"Same old Susie," Denis commented. "You've got a deal."

"Okay, Denis. I'll try to get back to you tomorrow. Where are you staying?"

"Hyatt Regency."

"Sacha with you?"

"Yes."

"Naughty boy. Call you tomorrow."

chapter
10

Edwin Earhart's problems with the bottle finally led to the loss of his position as head of the claims department at the Rock Island Railroad. Finding nothing better, he accepted a menial job as a freight clerk for the Great Northern Railway in St. Paul. Later, in search of a less demeaning position, Earhart moved the family to Springfield, Missouri, where a job he had been promised did not materialize.

Stranded, and with no immediate employment prospects for Earhart, the family decided to split up, at least temporarily. Edwin Earhart would seek adequate employment while his wife and two teenage daughters went to live in Chicago with the Shedds, who were friends of the family from Des Moines.

After they had settled in with the Shedds, schooling for the two Earhart girls became the priority issue. Muriel quickly enrolled in the nearby Morgan Park High School, but Amelia insisted on interviewing the principal and examining the school's facilities before she made her own decision. While the Morgan Park School may have been adequate for her sister, Amelia refused to go there. She had inspected the chemistry laboratory and concluded that it was nothing more than a "kitchen sink." Finally Amelia *chose the Hyde Park school, which had good courses in chemistry and physics, as well as a decent lab.*

Dr. Wilfred Lash led the small group of men into a comfortable room which contrasted sharply with the stark, hospital environment of the surrounding facilities. Inside, Colonel Cerilla, a member of the party, noticed two rows of stuffed armchairs all facing a curtained wall at the opposite end of the room. Pedestaled ashtrays were conveniently located by most of the chairs, for the benefit of doctors who chose not to follow their own advice. The place reminded Cerilla of a movie mogul's private screening room, although he had never seen one personally.

Dr. Lash invited the four other men to take seats in the front row. Apart from Cerilla, the rest of the group seemed cut from the same cloth, representative members of a single profession. All were in their late forties or fifties, wore glasses and conservative but wrinkled suits, and most appeared slightly overweight. Cerilla, a man in peak physical shape who wore his military demeanor like a badge of honor, contrasted markedly from his companions, although they shared a common purpose in assembling.

When everyone was seated, Dr. Lash stood before them and spoke.

"Gentlemen, in a few minutes we will proceed with the first direct examination of Mrs. Stenemond's claims. As you know, Mrs. Stenemond has already been subjected to a rigorous physical and physiognomical examination that leads us to believe that it is possible, and I repeat 'possible,' that she is Miss Earhart. You should also know that Mrs. Stenemond has twice asked to leave the Institute, but her physician, Dr. Wilton, has prevailed upon her to stay. We are still trying to locate any of Miss Earhart's dental records and fingerprints, and I believe, Colonel Cerilla, that your people are helping with that." Cerilla nodded, and Dr. Lash continued: "The ground rules for today's session are as follows: Dr. Gruber and Dr. Jensen will observe the questioning for psychological or parapsychological clues that may subsequently help us in evaluating Mrs. Stenemond's story. Obviously we've got to make darn sure that the whole thing isn't an elaborate hoax.

"Colonel Cerilla and Dr. Martin have prepared a series of substantive questions about Amelia Earhart which will test Mrs. Stenemond's knowledge of the subject. As agreed, in today's session we will confine the examination to Miss Earhart's childhood. Are there any questions?"

None of the men stirred, so Dr. Lash walked to the side of the curtained wall and grasped a drawstring. Before pulling it, he added: "Mrs. Stenemond's physician, Dr. Wilton, will induce a hypnotic trance prior to the questioning." Dr. Lash tugged at the string, drawing the curtains apart to reveal a floor-length tinted-glass window. Through the window the men viewed another room, this one more in keeping with hospital standards. It contained the normal paraphernalia of an examination room, and there in the center sat Mrs. Stenemond in a straight chair, as Dr. Wilton towered over her, preparing to induce the trance.

The four men seated in the armchairs gazed through the green-tinged glass while Dr. Lash walked to another corner of the room and picked up a long, cordless microphone that had been resting on a felt-covered table. "Dr. Martin and Colonel Cerilla will use this microphone to ask questions," Dr. Lash said. "Flip this red switch to turn it on. When the switch is not engaged, Mrs. Stenemond and Dr. Wilton will be unable to hear us. That may prove useful should it become necessary to comment on some of her replies. We will hear Mrs. Stenemond through the speakers encased in the wall over there." Lash pointed to the right of the glass wall. Then he flicked the microphone switch on and spoke into it. As he spoke, his voice reverberated throughout the room. "Dr. Wilton, is your subject in a trance?"

Wilton looked through the tinted glass and nodded.

"Thank you," Dr. Lash said. Then he raised his voice slightly. "Mrs. Stenemond, can you hear me?" The elderly woman nodded faintly. Lash continued: "Mrs. Stenemond, do you believe that you are Amelia Earhart?"

Cerilla started in awe at the woman, watching her reaction as the question registered in her mind. She wore the sort of clothes one would expect a seventy-eight-year-old woman to wear: a flowered chiffon dress with long sleeves and small rhinestone buttons fastened up to the neck. Cerilla wondered how many pictures of Amelia Earhart he had seen in his career. Hundreds, no doubt. Now he tried to remember all of them as he superimposed the photographs and an additional forty years on the woman before him. Mrs. Stenemond's bone structure bore enough resemblance to Cerilla's composite mental photograph to pass muster. The hair was no longer tousled, but short and gray. From this distance, Cerilla could not see Mrs. Stenemond's eyes.

Mrs. Stenemond looked up, gazed at the glass partition, and in a female voice whose timbre reflected maturity and confidence, she said: "Yes, I am Amelia Earhart."

"Very well, Mrs. Stenemond," Lash said. "Dr. Martin would like to ask you a few questions."

Lash walked over to Martin's armchair and gave him the microphone. Martin had a kindly face and ample girth, the sort of man who, with beard and costume, would make an ideal Santa Claus. He cleared his throat and asked several "easy" questions related to Amelia Earhart's childhood in Kansas. Mrs. Stenemond replied accurately and without hesitation. Dr. Martin then proceeded to his more difficult set of questions.

"Miss Earhart, in what year did you graduate from high school?"

"In 1916," Mrs. Stenemond replied.

"Do you recall the name of the high school?"

"Certainly. The Hyde Park High School in Chicago. I remember that my mother and sister and I were living with some friends in Chicago at the time."

"What was the name of the family with whom you were living?"

"The ... uh ... the Shedds. Yes, the Shedds."

Dr. Martin switched off the microphone and addressed

his colleagues. "Everything she said is absolutely true." He handed the microphone to Cerilla.

Dr. Gruber, who had remained silent, suddenly perked up and spoke in an agitated German accent. "But all of that information can be learned, correct? There is nothing secret about it."

"You are right, so far," Dr. Martin conceded, "but to suggest that Mrs. Stenemond learned all of this information is to subscribe to the theory that this is all a monstrous hoax."

"Not necessarily," Dr. Gruber rejoined in a high-pitched, professional tone. "The subject might be highly influenced by an experience in her youth. Perhaps she was fascinated by the legend of Miss Earhart and read books about her. Such experiences can trigger identification trauma, where the subject subsequently becomes, subconsciously at least, the object of her fantasy."

"If I may say something," Cerilla offered cautiously, "the questions I have prepared for Mrs. Stenemond are few, but they involve such detail about Miss Earhart's childhood that it is not likely that anyone but Amelia Earhart herself could answer them all. May I proceed?"

Dr. Lash nodded, and Cerilla switched the microphone on. Mrs. Stenemond, her physician standing alongside, waited attentively for the question.

"Miss, uh, Earhart," Cerilla began, "when you were a little girl in Kansas, you had a pet dog who meant a great deal to you. Do you recall that?"

"Oh, yes," Mrs. Stenemond replied, her voice suddenly rhapsodic.

"Would you happen to recall the dog's name?"

"Yes, sir. I could never forget him. We called him—oh, it was such a funny name!—we called him James Ferocious." Mrs. Stenemond giggled girlishly as she said it.

The men behind the glass partition looked toward Cerilla, who acknowledged with a nod that the answer was correct.

"Miss Earhart," Cerilla continued, pressing the microphone to his lips as he gazed at her through the glass, "in your senior year in high school, you got A's in only two subjects. Which were they?"

"Oh, that question is not difficult, sir. I earned A's in chemistry and physics." Then Mrs. Stenemond added in a chiding tone: "And not just my senior year, either!"

Cerilla again acknowledged to his colleagues and to Dr. Wilton that Mrs. Stenemond's answer was correct.

"One last question, Miss Earhart," Cerilla continued. "And, frankly, it's possible you won't know the answer to this one. But do you happen to recall the caption under your photograph in the Hyde Park High School yearbook in 1916?"

Mrs. Stenemond looked quizzically in the direction of the glass partition, as if wondering why these strange people were asking all of these silly questions. "That is a difficult question, sir," she said, "and I don't recall . . . Let me think . . . No, I cannot remember." Mrs. Stenemond then turned to her physician. "Please, may I go now? I beg you again. Please let me leave. . . ." The old woman's voice was strained.

Dr. Martin spoke into the microphone and addressed his colleague in the other room. "Your patient seems very upset, Doctor. Perhaps this has all been too much of an ordeal for her."

Dr. Wilton's terse reply came over the speaker. "I know my patient, Doctor. And I will decide on her ability to sustain the examinations."

"No doubt. But I don't have to be her personal physician to understand in plain English that she wants to leave! My question, Doctor, is the following: Are you detaining that woman here against her will?"

Cerilla interjected himself into the discussion in an attempt to head off a professional squabble. "Dr. Wilton, would you excuse us for a moment?"

Cerilla clicked off the microphone.

Dr. Louis Martin motioned to Dr. Lash that he wanted to speak. "I think we ought to get one matter out on the table right now," Martin said firmly. "That woman wants to go home, and it seems to me her doctor won't let her."

"He is her doctor, though. And he is professionally qualified," Lash pointed out.

"Well, I have my doubts about that," Martin continued. "There's a rumor around the Institute that Dr. Wilton has contracted with a magazine for the Earhart story and that's why he's making her go on with these tests. They say he won't make a cent unless he can prove that she's real."

"Oh, for God's sake, Lou," Dr. Lash said. "I've heard those rumors, too. I even asked Wilton about them, if you must know. He denied all of it, and that's probably why he's so touchy about his relationship with his patient."

Martin rejoined at once, "Well, I just want everyone here to know that I will not be a party to that woman's being kept here against her will."

"Neither will any of us, Lou," Dr. Lash concurred. "Look, if it makes you feel better, I'll ask Wilton to allow you to speak to her privately. All right?"

Dr. Martin nodded.

"Good. Now, let's get back to the main question: Is it possible that Mrs. Stenemond is Amelia Earhart? Let's each of us give his opinion in turn. If there is a clear consensus, we can then issue a statement about our findings. We might as well start with you, Lou."

"Well," Dr. Martin began as he straightened himself in the armchair, "I must say I'm impressed, truly impressed. The evidence here is not conclusive, of course, but the details of this woman's recollections are extraordinary. Frankly, I believe she could be Amelia Earhart."

Dr. Jensen, who was invited to speak next, echoed his colleague's impressions and offered his opinion that the knowledge of such detail could only be the result of having lived through the experience.

Dr. Gruber, whose frown had generated an increasing number of wrinkles as his colleagues spoke, finally took the floor. "I am not convinced," he stated authoritatively.

"Well, none of us is certain," Dr. Lash interjected, "but

we're merely stating that we are impressed with the evidence so far."

"I too am impressed," Gruber boomed. "But I am impressed principally by Mrs. Stenemond's feat of memory." Gruber rose and faced his colleagues. He spread his arms, as if to confer a blessing or begin a lecture, which were synonymous benefits in his estimation. Cerilla watched silently, harboring his own thoughts.

"Gentlemen," Gruber began, "let us not get carried away! I implore you to view this matter critically and objectively.

"Assume for a minute that Mrs. Stenemond is not Amelia Earhart. In that case, she is either a well-trained fraud or she is the victim of subconscious psychological self-delusion. In both cases, she could know many details of Amelia Earhart's life, either because she had been trained to remember them or because she read about and was influenced by them in her childhood.

"Her knowledge is indeed impressive, gentlemen, but, I repeat, it could have been learned. Note carefully that she did not know the answer to Colonel Cerilla's final question. Personally, I find that quite significant."

While Gruber spoke, Dr. Martin allowed his eyes to wander back to the glass, through which he saw Mrs. Stenemond, sitting quietly on the chair, her arms folded in her lap.

Dr. Lash nodded pensively. "I think Dr. Gruber has a point. If Mrs. Stenemond could remember so many other details of her high-school days, why could she not recall her own yearbook caption?"

Dr. Martin protested. "For God's sake, the woman is almost eighty years old! Do any of you remember your yearbook captions?"

"We didn't have captions," Dr. Jensen retorted.

"Nor did we," Dr. Gruber said.

"I remember mine," Dr. Lash admitted, "but I'll spare you the recitation." Lash then addressed Colonel Cerilla. "Say, Colonel, where did you dig up these questions?"

"All of them were researched from published material,

her biography, her sister's book, various sources. All, that is, except one question."

"Which one, Colonel?" Lash asked.

"The question about the caption. We got that from the high school directly."

"You see!" Dr. Gruber exclaimed. "The one question she did not know is the one question that is not from a book!"

"It might be in a book," Cerilla pointed out. "We just didn't find it there."

But as he surveyed his colleagues' reactions, it became clear to Gruber that he was winning some converts to the side of skepticism.

Suddenly the speakers on the wall crackled, calling everyone's attention to the forgotten people on the other side of the glass partition. Mrs. Stenemond's voice echoed in the room.

"The girl in brown who walks alone," she said.

"What the hell does that mean?" Lash asked.

Colonel Cerilla stood up and replied in a sober tone. "It may mean, Doctor, that your latest theory has gone up in smoke. Mrs. Stenemond just recited the yearbook caption."

chapter
11

The first leg of Amelia Earhart's trip may have portended later trouble, because virtually nothing went wrong, an ominous occurrence that long-distance pilots distrusted.

Upon arrival in Hawaii, Mantz disembarked, and Amelia wanted to leave again within a few hours, but a storm forced a day's postponement. The delay allowed Amelia to spend the day on Waikiki Beach, visiting with Mantz and his fiancée, a Honolulu resident.

The following morning, at daybreak, Earhart, Manning, and Fred Noonan climbed into the Electra and prepared for takeoff. Amelia took the controls and began to roll down the three thousand feet of concrete runway.

Almost immediately she sensed something was wrong. Within seconds, as they sped down the runway, Amelia's suspicions were confirmed. They were not generating enough speed to take off.

Suddenly the plane veered to one side. Amelia, reacting instinctively, throttled back on one engine, which caused the aircraft to spin off the runway, damaging the landing gear and wing. As she lost control, Amelia calmly cut the switches, possibly preventing a fire. Fortunately, no one was hurt, and although the precise cause of the crash was never determined, it was obvious that the flight could not continue. The Electra would require complete repair and overhaul on the mainland, a job that would take several months. Reporters swarmed around the aviators as they made their way back to the hangar, and the obvious question was for Amelia: Will you give up or go ahead? Amelia stopped, turned toward the press entourage, and told them firmly: "Of course I shall try again!"

The morning sun streamed through the venetian blinds in the hotel room, casting gray shadowed stripes on the two nude bodies in the bed. Deep in the entanglements of their lovemaking, Denis and Sacha whispered, renewing vows of devotion and commitment to one another.

The phone rang, jarring the silent atmosphere and terminating prematurely the couple's physical activities.

"Damn," Denis muttered as he rolled over and picked up the phone on the third shrill ring. It was Susie Mitchell from Washington.

"Hi, sport. Did I catch you at a bad moment?" she said cheerfully. "Seems to me I have a vague recollection about your morning perversions."

Denis grumbled something unintelligible, in lieu of a witty reply, which he couldn't conjure up on the moment. While they spoke, Sacha sat up in bed, scowling at the thought of Susie's unfortunate timing. *She must have known somehow*, Sacha thought. *That bitch.*

"Well, I've got some news for you," Susie said, while Denis propped the phone to his ear with his shoulder and prepared to take notes in his reporter's pad.

"Let's hear it, Susie," Denis said, his pencil poised and ready for action.

"My best source at the Pentagon—and don't ask me who it is—will normally tell me just about anything short of our plans for World War Three. But soon after I mentioned the *Sherman*, he clammed up tighter than a cat's ass.

I couldn't believe it! Information on *Sherman* survivors? No way, he said. Highest security classification. Looks like you're on to something, Denis."

"Yeah," Denis said, his voice reflecting the disappointment of Susie's news. "Thanks anyway."

"Wait, I'm not finished. Deep in the Pentagon," she went on, "is a little-known two-room office called the Department of Disabled Personnel. All they do is channel complaints or answer inquiries from disabled veterans who feel they're getting the runaround. Well, in there, my friend, I struck paydirt."

As Denis scribbled furiously, Susie recounted the story of how she had used a source within the Department to find out how many sailors who went on disability in the late thirties were still alive. Susie's pretext was that she was writing a feature on pre-World War Two Navy veterans. The cooperative source searched some of the more recent records, plowing through stacks of correspondence as part of the exercise, and came up with a handful of possibilities. There were all sorts of complaints, about poor military facilities, uncooperative staff personnel, and mostly about lost or misplaced benefits checks.

As discreetly as possible, Susie asked to see some of the correspondence. Since none of it was classified, the source was happy to cooperate.

"In that stack of correspondence," Susie said, "I found a *Sherman* survivor."

He had written to the Pentagon for help with a problem. His benefits checks were frequently delayed, and although he had complained several times through normal channels, the delays had persisted. In keeping with his military training, William Kinderman duly noted in his letter his service number, Social Security number, and the details of his disability. He had been wounded in a ship explosion in 1937. His ship had been the USS *Sherman*.

"Where does he live?" Denis asked, his hand now aching from the frenetic writing.

"Houston, Texas."

"Phone number?"

"Look it up. I've done enough for you for one day."

"You sure have, Susie. Many thanks. I'll live up to my end of the bargain."

When the conversation ended, Sacha poked Denis in the midsection and murmured accusingly: "I'll bet I can guess what your end of the bargain is."

Denis smiled and patted her behind. "Not what you're thinking, honey. She wants something much more valuable than that."

Denis glanced at his watch on the bedside table—9:30. He decided to try to reach Mr. William Kinderman. Sacha watched as Denis made a move for the phone. She rose from the bed and ran a hand through her long blond hair. "Well, I guess I'll take a cold shower. Looks like there isn't anything going on out here." Her perfectly contoured nude body formed a statuesque, shadowy shape against the hazy daylight seeping in from the blinds.

Denis replaced the receiver. "Shit. I don't know the area code for Houston."

"Seven-one-three," Sacha obliged.

Denis looked up at her. "How did you know that?"

Sacha walked toward the bathroom, and before entering she turned around. "You're not the only one with a past, you know." She went in and closed the door.

Denis shook his head and dialed the information number for Houston. An operator with a king-sized drawl was happy to help. Yes, there was a listing for a Mr. William Kinderman. Denis took it down, offered his thanks, pressed the plunger, and this time dialed Mr. Kinderman's area code and number.

A man answered on the second ring. Denis identified himself, without mentioning his occupation, and asked Kinderman if he had recently written to the Pentagon about his benefits.

"Sure did," said the gravelly voice, obviously an elderly man. "Glad you called about it, too. I suppose you're the fellow who's going to fix it up."

"I just need to ask you a few background questions, Mr. Kinderman. Please bear with me." As he spoke, Denis heard the shower start up in the bathroom, and he hoped the sound would not be transmitted over the Bell System to Texas.

"It's okay, sonny. I'm used to government procedures."

"Fine, Mr. Kinderman. Let's see, now, you became disabled in 1937, is that right?"

"Correct."

"And you were on the USS *Sherman*."

"That's right."

"Tell me, Mr. Kinderman, do you remember any of the circumstances surrounding the *Sherman*'s disappearance?"

The voice in Texas suddenly became silent. Denis waited three interminable seconds and asked: "Mr. Kinderman, are you still there?"

"I'm here," he replied, in a tone approaching hostility. "Are you sure you work for the government?"

"I never said I did. I'm a reporter for the New York *Daily Press*."

"A reporter! I can't talk to you."

"Wait, Mr. Kinderman," Denis shouted. "Don't hang up. Why can't you talk to me?"

"I just can't, that's all. Orders."

"Whose orders?"

"I can't say."

"Well, listen carefully, Mr. Kinderman"—Denis' voice now assuming an edge—"you've already talked to me and I need some more questions answered."

"You tricked me."

"I'll tell you what," Denis said, "if you answer my questions, I promise I won't reveal your name. You'll be fully protected."

Kinderman grunted and Denis could almost hear the rusty wheels churning in his mind. "What if I don't?"

Denis took a deep breath. "If you refuse to answer my questions, Mr. Kinderman, I'm going to identify you as a

Sherman survivor and you'll be able to read your name tomorrow morning in every newspaper in the country."

"Oh, God," the old man exclaimed. Then he sighed. "Okay, mister. Ask your questions, and you be damn sure you never mention my name."

Denis quickly assumed his reportorial role, posing questions, following up on inadequate answers, bearing down to eke out the last ounce of knowledge possessed by his interviewee. Unfortunately, Kinderman knew very little. He had been a machinist on the *Sherman*, and spent most of his time below deck. He had not seen Amelia Earhart, knew nothing of the *Sherman's* cargo and, as a Houston resident, had not read Denis' article on the subject.

"Were all the survivors below deck when the ship exploded?" Denis asked.

"I dunno. I guess so. . . . No, one sailor was on the bridge, I remember that now."

"What's his name?"

"Carnoff. Jason Carnoff. We were in the VA Hospital in San Francisco together. They sent us there after we were picked up. Jesus, those Pentagon guys gave him a workover."

"Do you know where he is now?"

"Nope. Never saw him again. Not since 1937."

"Well, thanks, Mr. Kinderman," Denis said, as he wrote down Carnoff's name and then stretched his fingers to relieve the writer's cramp. "I may call you again, but that's all the questions I have for you now."

Denis crumpled a blank piece of paper on his pad and took aim at the wastebasket across the room.

"Uh, young man," Kinderman said into the phone.

"Yes, Mr. Kinderman." Denis launched the paper wad. Swish. One thousand nine hundred and forty.

"Do you think you might be able to do something about my disability checks?"

chapter
12

In 1920 the Earharts lived in a frame house in downtown Los Angeles. Edwin Earhart, now a converted Christian Scientist, had renounced liquor and begun to build up a private law practice. To help make ends meet, they took boarders in their large house, one of whom was a young engineer, Sam Chapman. Chapman displayed an early romantic interest in Amelia, and they seemed to enjoy each other's company. But when the conversation turned to the serious topic of marriage, Amelia would invariably change the subject.

One day Sam Chapman introduced a friend, Peter Barnes, to the Earharts. Barnes had bought the rights to a gypsum mine in Nevada, but he lacked the capital to develop it. After investigating the mine's potential, the Earharts decided to invest their remaining twenty thousand dollars in the venture, hoping thereby to rebuild their fortunes. Edwin Earhart and Amelia went to visit Barnes at the mine on a day when the Indian workers had refused to report to work; they feared the effect of floods on that early-winter morning. Barnes ignored their pleas and insisted that the work must go on. But the rains came, quickly filling the gullies and crevices of the mountainside mine.

Soon powerful rivers had formed and were swirling around everywhere. Edwin and Amelia made it safely across a rickety bridge, but Barnes, who followed closely behind, was swept away in a powerful current. His dead body was recovered the following day.

The Veterans Administration Hospital in San Francisco resembled a medieval fortress whose massive stone structure had darkened with age, the weatherbeaten victim of Pacific storms and the merciless rays of the sun. Looking at it, Denis mentally supplied a moat and drawbridge.

Inside, Denis flashed his press credentials and spun a concocted tale about an article he was writing on pre-World War Two sailors. The hospital's assistant administrator, James Farrell, a cherubic middle-aged man, listened attentively, and raised his eyebrows only twice while listening to Denis' story. He checked the credentials again, then led Denis to the Records Room, an aptly named storage area with wall-to-wall filing cabinets on one side and a complete Microfilm-viewing setup on the other.

"You understand, Mr. Keyser," Farrell said solemnly, "that I can't show you the complete medical records of any individual. Only the admissions file. Regulations, you know."

"I understand perfectly," Denis said. "Now, if I could have the admissions records for 1936, 1937, and 1938, that might be a good start."

Farrell blinked and waddled over to the microfilm section. He rummaged through one of the drawers, talking to himself all the while. "Let's see . . . 1936, '37, and '38 . . . Aha, here we are!" He handed Denis three microfilm files with a flourish.

"Thank you, Mr. Farrell," Denis said, sensing a victory. "I think I can handle it from here."

"Well, let me show you how these machines work," Farrell said gingerly. He walked over to the viewing machine and inserted one of the films. Farrell then proceeded to explain the machine's operation at excessive length while

Denis resisted telling him that he could field-strip one of those things and put it back together in less than forty-two seconds. Farrell finally finished his discourse, and, to Denis' relief, the rotund man headed for the door.

At last, Denis thought. He switched the machine on and inserted the 1937 film. Spinning the film-advance knob rapidly, he skipped through several months of patient admissions in a quick blur. The records were organized alphabetically by date, so Denis picked July 13 as a starting point. He reasoned that if the *Sherman* had gone down the same day as Amelia Earhart was lost, it would have taken at least ten days for the survivors to be discovered and then transferred to the hospital in San Francisco.

Denis scanned the letter C for the thirteenth. Nothing. The fourteenth yielded no better results. Finally, on the listings for July 15, 1937, Denis found the entry:

Carnoff, Jason
Svc nbr: 5642981
Branch: Navy
Last assignment: Assistant radio operator,
USS *Sherman*
Date of birth: 4/5/20
Next of kin: NCA
Home address: NCA

Damn, Denis thought. Got to get Farrell back in the act. Resigned, he rose and went to the door.

"Mr. Farrell!" Denis yelled.

Farrell emerged from a nearby doorway. "Yes?"

"What does NCA mean after an entry?"

"Not currently available," Farrell obliged.

"Why wouldn't a man's home address be available?"

"Sometimes people are admitted here unconscious and we can't get the information right then. Of course, we run things much better nowadays, and if that happened we would go back and complete the record. But in the 1930s . . ." Farrell shrugged.

"I see," Denis said. He looked intently at the chubby man. "Say, Farrell . . . I just may be able to do a little feature on you as part of this story. You know, the man behind the scenes at a big hospital. That kind of thing."

A blush formed on Farrell's face. "Oh, that's not really necessary," he said, as if he had just invented false modesty.

"However, I could use some more information on the patients," Denis continued. "Do you have any personnel on the staff who were here in 1937?"

"Forty years ago?" Farrell mulled it over. "Let's see: there's Jake Townsend. Oh, dear me, no. He started right after the war." Farrell scratched his balding head. "Gosh, I really couldn't say."

"Anyone you can ask?" Denis persisted.

Farrell frowned, lost in thought. Then he looked up and beamed. "I could ask Mary, my secretary. She's been here almost thirty years. Maybe she'd know . . . I'll be right back."

Farrell disappeared, leaving Denis alone in the room with the machine, on whose screen Jason Carnoff's vital data glowed. Within three minutes Farrell was back.

"Two nurses," he announced. "We have two nurses on the staff who started over forty years ago. I've sent for them."

Moments later, one of the nurses, Liz Bollo, arrived, and Farrell introduced her, then discreetly left the room. Denis spun his well-rehearsed tale about the newspaper story he was writing and asked the matronly woman various questions about her early career. He soon learned that Mrs. Bollo did not remember a Jason Carnoff, which wasn't all that surprising, since she had worked in the hospital pharmacy and had had little contact with patients.

When Mrs. Bollo had returned to her duties, Farrell rejoined Denis in the Records Room, where they chatted aimlessly until they were interrupted by a knock on the door. Rose Johnson, a registered nurse who Farrell had said was recently widowed, opened the door and entered timidly. She was tall for a woman and her perfect posture accentuated her height. Mrs. Johnson had gray-white hair and a statuesque elegance about her.

"You called for me, Mr. Farrell," she asked, a touch of anxiety in her voice.

"Yes, Rose. I want you to meet Mr. Denis Keyser, of the New York *Daily Press*," Farrell said. "He'd like to chat with you for a few minutes. Just let me know when you're through." Farrell beamed at Denis and left.

Denis stood to shake Mrs. Johnson's hand, which she tendered after wiping it perfunctorily on her white uniform. He took her for a woman of about sixty, whose face and eyes had endured the aging process with dignity and grace.

"Please sit down, Mrs. Johnson," Denis said kindly, sensing the woman's unease. "As I explained to Mr. Farrell, I'm doing an article for my paper and I need to chat with people who were here in the hospital a long time ago. Were you working here in 1937?"

Mrs. Johnson's eyes sparkled as she answered. "That's the very year I started, Mr. Keyser," she said wistfully. "I was eighteen years old at the time."

"We're building the story around one or two men," Denis continued. "Do you happen to remember a patient— a sailor—named Jason Carnoff?"

Her eyes widened. "Oh, yes. Have you heard from Jason? I would dearly love to have news of him. It's been so long . . ."

Denis fumbled with his reporter's pad to conceal his excitement. "So you know Jason Carnoff."

Mrs. Johnson smiled shyly. "I knew all my patients—and I remember them well—but Jason was more than just a patient to me."

Denis leaned forward. "Do go on, Mrs. Johnson. Please."

The stately nurse sighed. "You see, Jason was my first beau." Mrs. Johnson explained that as Rose Mullen, her maiden name, she had attended to the young sailor for several months. With the passage of time, the young woman had become captivated by Jason's tenderness and sensitivity, and she comforted him following his grueling sessions with the interrogators from Washington and his frequent nightmares over the loss of a drowned colleague. As romances go, this one had few of the ingredients of a torrid gothic novel. Jason was confined to bed and Rose spent many of her off-duty hours sitting by his side, holding his hand, whispering thoughts born of dreams and fantasies.

"I think those men from Washington shook him to his roots," Mrs. Johnson continued. "Jason was so afraid of them."

"Mrs. Johnson," Denis asked gently, mindful of the soft femininity of this graceful woman, "did you keep in touch with Jason?"

"No," she said, her eyes melancholic. "And that was so strange. We had planned to correspond regularly after his discharge, but I received only one letter—Jason wrote to tell me that he wanted to get away from his past for a while. But I never heard from him again." She shook her head sadly. "We were so close, Mr. Keyser. I was deeply hurt that Jason didn't write. I know he was sincere about his feelings for me, but I never understood why he ran away without telling me."

Denis let the comment pass and asked softly: "Do you know where he went after he left San Francisco?"

"The one letter he sent me was from Des Moines, Iowa."

"Was Jason from Iowa?"

"No, Jason was raised somewhere in Pennsylvania. He never wanted to talk much about his childhood. I assumed it was not a pleasant one."

Denis turned the information over in his mind. He had learned precious little, but the interview had provided one geographic lead: Des Moines, Iowa.

"Thank you, Mrs. Johnson," Denis said, as he closed his notepad. "I really appreciate your talking to me."

Mrs. Johnson rose to leave. When she reached the door

she turned to Denis and said: "If you find Jason, Mr. Keyser, for whatever reason you're looking for him, will you please tell him I asked about him?"

"I certainly will," Denis said. "Thanks again."

Sacha was gabbing on the phone when Denis unlocked the door to their hotel room. She waved at him, finished her conversation, and hung up.

"I've got a super job next week," she boasted as she sprang up to kiss Denis on the cheek. "A photo assignment for Vogue."

" 'Bout time they discovered you. I always knew I had good taste."

Denis removed his jacket and tossed it on the bed, plopped into an armchair, and closed his eyes, trying to relax.

"Poor baby," Sacha said. "You've had a rough day, haven't you? How did you make out?"

"Only fair." Denis sighed. He opened his eyes and sat up. "Say, in your reservoir of phone numbers you don't happen to have the area code for Des Moines, Iowa, do you?"

"Five-one-five," Sacha replied instantly.

Denis raised an eyebrow but refrained from asking her how she knew it, lest the conversation degenerate into a spot quiz on old flames. That kind of discussion, he knew, never ended harmoniously.

"Honey, would you mind calling information in Des Moines and asking for the number of a Jason Carnoff. That's C-a-r-n-o-f-f."

Sacha nodded and dialed the phone while Denis sat quietly, occasionally rubbing his eyes to relieve the strain. He heard Sacha spell the name for the operator, wait a few seconds, and hang up. "There's no such listing, Denis," she said.

"I was afraid of that."

"What do we do now?"

"Well," Denis said, unwinding slowly from the armchair, "this afternoon I'll attend the press conference at the Medical Institute. The word's already leaked that those doctors are impressed as hell with Mrs. Stenemond. They think she might actually be Amelia Earhart, but they're not sure yet."

"Then what?"

"I file my story with the paper, and then we leave."

"You know, it'll be kind of nice to get back to New York." Sacha smiled. "San Francisco's beautiful and all, but it doesn't seem to vibrate and excite me like the Big Apple."

"We're not going to New York," Denis announced.

Sacha looked at him in surprise.

Denis flung his arms wide and continued in a voice full of loud mock enthusiasm. "Because, my darling, we are off to Des Moines, capital of that great state of Iowa, in the rolling plains—"

"But, Denis!" Sacha protested.

"Don't worry," Denis said reassuringly, this time in his normal voice. "I'll get you back in plenty of time to dazzle the editors at Vogue."

chapter
13

Work on the Electra proceeded at a frantic pace, and less than two months after the Honolulu crack-up, the aircraft was repaired and airworthy. On May 20, 1937, the 'round-the-world flight got under way from Oakland, California, once again shrouded in secrecy. The plan called for a flight to Miami, where Pan Am technicians would give it a final workover, then on to points east: Puerto Rico, Brazil, Africa, Burma, Singapore, Australia, Howland Island, Hawaii, and back to Oakland.

In order to help finance the trip, Amelia carried along a box of airmail covers, envelopes that would be canceled at various stops along the way and later sold by a department store in New York at a considerable profit.

When Paul Mantz, who had traveled on the fateful flight to Honolulu, learned of Amelia's departure, he was furious, and accused Putnam of rushing the flight in order to satisfy radio and advertising commitments. Mantz had wanted to check Amelia's radio again before her departure, since its functioning had not satisfied him on the previous flight. But by then, Earhart and Noonan had already arrived in Miami.

The Pan Am technicians worked on the plane for a week

under the hot Florida sun. On June 7, at daybreak, Earhart and Noonan took their places in the silver aircraft. Putnam was there to see his wife off. Just before six a.m. the Electra streaked off into the clear, warm sky, taking its crew from the shores of the United States on a voyage they would never complete.

A brisk summer wind swirled around the docks under a cloudy sky, and Peggy shivered.

"I should have brought a sweater," she lamented.

Without saying a word, Jason removed his jacket and drapped it around Peggy's shoulders as they continued to walk along the pier. Overhead, seagulls swarmed around aimlessly and the air was filled with the aroma of the sea.

They passed several yachts berthed at right angles to the pier and Jason wished that their upcoming journey could be in one of those wood-lined floating palaces that seemed so inviting. No matter. If his mission was successful, he knew that he could afford any yacht in the world.

"It should be just ahead," Jason said reassuringly as he put his arm around Peggy's waist, helping her along. After another two minutes' walk, their land journey was over: the *Princess* lay just before them.

She was larger than Jason had imagined, a 190-foot gleaming white, steel-hulled ship which had previously served as a Coast Guard buoy tender. Soapy Denton had had her refitted with powerful new engines, and installed all the paraphernalia of diving in her bowels and on her decks, making the *Princess* the best-equipped salvage ship in the world. Jacques Cousteau had inspected her once and commented afterward that his *Calypso* seemed like a rowboat by comparison. Denton had used the *Princess* on all of his most recent salvage missions, including the spectacular raising of the USS *Grant*, a nuclear-powered submarine that sank mysteriously off the coast of Spain, taking 124 American lives down with her. The great salvage companies of the world had been approached by the U.S. Navy in an effort to raise the *Grant* and recover her nuclear weapons. One by one, they had refused, stating that the job was virtually impossible. Only Soapy Denton had had the sheer nerve to attempt the task, and against all the odds, Denton succeeded, establishing himself as the best underwater expert in the business.

Peggy joined Jason in staring in awe at the ship. "What's all the stuff on deck?" she asked.

Jason reached far back in his memory and had surprisingly little difficulty recalling his past naval experience.

"That contraption on the aft deck is an air compressor," Jason said. "They use it for diving. And next to it . . . I suspect that's an auxiliary generating plant."

"Right you are!" boomed Soapy Denton as he joined them them from behind, causing them to jump. He wore a crumpled white captain's hat and a bold blue-and-white-striped shirt. "This is the best-equipped salvage ship in the world." Denton let loose a wide proud grin. "And it's going to be your home for the next few weeks. Maybe longer. I've got a nice cabin picked out for you. Say, where's your luggage?"

"We left it at the gatehouse," Peggy said, pointing toward the end of the pier. "We couldn't carry the bags this far."

"No problem," Denton replied. "I'll send one of the crew for it. C'mon aboard."

They climbed the shaky gangplank single file and as soon as they were on deck Jason felt the familiar vibration of the ship's engines. They lowered their heads to follow Soapy through an oval doorway and proceeded through a maze of narrow corridors to the open door of the cabin Soapy had selected for them.

"It's got its own private facilities," Soapy boasted. "What do you think?"

Peggy smiled. "It's a lot better than I thought it would be," she commented with a tone of relief as she took in the sight of the small cabin. It had two small beds, side by side, a desk and chair, and a single stuffed armchair. Old framed prints on the wall told of epic sea battles in the days when ships were powered by huge fluffy sails. Sunlight streamed through two brass-encased portholes at the far end of the cabin.

"It'll be just fine, Soapy," Peggy said, and she sincerely meant it.

"Good. The bags'll be up in a second. How about a tour of the ship?"

Peggy settled comfortably in the armchair. "You two go ahead," she said. "I'll stay here and unpack."

Jason and Soapy wandered through the ship, occasionally stopping to chat with a sailor, a diver, and finally the cook, a rotund Belgian who promised that the culinary fare would rival the delights of the defunct *France*, on which he had served as an apprentice chef. On deck, Soapy pointed out the machine shop, a fully equipped facility for the repair and maintenance of compressors, winches, and diving equipment, without which an equipment breakdown would force a time-consuming and expensive return to port for repairs. Beside the machine shop, a flying-saucer-type contraption was anchored to the deck.

As they stood nearby, the wind rustling through their clothes, Jason gazed at the infinite expanse of the Pacific Ocean rippling before him. He wondered if the idea of finding a single ship, the equivalent of a speck of sand in that massive body of water, made any sense at all.

Jason turned to Soapy and leaned against the railing. The purring of the engines served as a reminder that their departure was now imminent. "How will we search for the ship once we get to the atoll?" Jason asked.

"We'll 'mag' for it," Soapy said matter-of-factly.

" 'Mag'?"

"Yeah. I've got the most sensitive magnometer ever developed. We drag it on a line at the bottom and it'll pick up iron or steel at forty feet. Then we use this two-man saucer sub. I'll show you how it all works when we get there."

Jason nodded and walked slowly toward the midship doorway to the ship's interior. Around them sailors shouted orders, uncoiled thick ropes, and made preparations for their departure. Soapy surveyed the activity in quick bursts of attention. Satisfied that the departure routine had proceeded smoothly, he cupped his hands to his mouth and shouted: "Okay, everybody. Next stop: Honolulu!"

Denis sipped his coffee and gazed out the window of the Rainbow Coffee Shoppe. A stream of pedestrians diverted his attention as he compared the attire of the citizens of Des Moines with the dress of the trendy, with-it New Yorkers. To Denis, Iowans seemed overweight as a class and displayed a decided preference for bright colors, checkered trousers, and double-knit fabrics.

Sacha burst into the place, conscious that she was twenty minutes late. Several men at the counter glanced her way, confirming that the sight of a New York fashion model was a rare treat in Des Moines.

"I'm sorry, I'm sorry, I'm sorry," Sacha said, and having dispensed with the three obligatory *mea culpas*, she took her seat at Denis' table. Sacha wore a tan jumpsuit, unzipped to the legal limit. She removed her sunglasses and leaned over the table to kiss Denis on the cheek. "Don't look so glum. I'm here."

"No problem. I like the coffee at this place."

"Well, let's get some for me." Sacha motioned to a waitress with a king-size beehive hairdo. She took the order for coffee and disappeared.

"How did you make out?" Sacha asked.

"Lousy. I couldn't find a Carnoff anywhere."

"Did you try the tax rolls?"

"Obviously," Denis replied, a touch irritated.

"Real-estate transfers, voter registration?"

"Hey, I'm the investigative reporter, remember? I do all that stuff in my sleep."

"Did you sleep okay last night?"

"You know damn well I did. C'mon, Sacha. I'm not in the mood for games."

The coffee arrived and Sacha took a sip. Two men at the

counter took turns looking around at her and commenting *sotto voce*. "Well," she said, "I did my chores. I checked the marriage licenses at City Hall, and no Carnoffs have been married here in the last forty years."

"Shit. We're at a dead end."

Sacha grinned. "I didn't say that, chum. You did."

"What are you talking about, Sacha?"

"Well, I may not be an investigative reporter or anything like that, but while I was at City Hall it occurred to me that if I were running away from my past, there's something else I might do besides go to Des Moines, Iowa."

Denis stared at her for a moment, and suddenly his eyes lit up in revelation. "My God, of course!"

Sacha beamed a smile of self-satisfaction. "So while I was at City Hall, I checked the court register of name changes. Sure enough, in 1938 Mr. Jason Carnoff changed his name to Jason Caldwell."

Denis looked into her eyes with feigned seriousness. "I always knew, deep down, that I loved you for more than your good looks."

Sacha smirked and ever-so-discreetly flashed her middle finger at Denis at tabletop level.

"Back to business," Denis said as he reached over and patted Sacha's expressive hand. "I suppose now we'll have to start the search all over again."

"Nope. The court records showed that Mr. Caldwell was employed by a Wall Street brokerage firm in their Des Moines office. So I went over there."

"You found him!" Denis shouted.

"'Fraid not. It seems Mr. Caldwell got himself transferred to the New York headquarters some years back."

"Okay, so we'll get him in New York. Anybody worth talking to here?"

"I don't think so. It's interesting, though. Those who do remember Caldwell say his departure was a complete surprise. He was being considered for the office manager's job when he suddenly decided he didn't want it and then asked for the transfer."

Denis signaled for the check. "Some people can't take responsibility," he commented. "Anyway, I'm glad we don't have to spend any more time here."

Sacha grinned and said sarcastically: "Don't worry, my dear. I'll get you back to New York in plenty of time to dazzle your editors at the *Press*."

chapter
14

As the Electra winged toward San Juan, Puerto Rico, Miami radio station WQAM reported that Amelia Earhart had embarked on her long-anticipated around-the-world flight. Amelia smiled as she monitored the broadcast, pleased and satisfied that she had managed to sneak away, avoiding the hassle of curious airport crowds and flocks of reporters.

The world lay before her now, a world she would attempt to encircle at the equator, a feat which had not yet been attempted by any pilot. But as she pushed the throttle forward, Amelia also moved inexorably closer to her personal rendezvous with destiny, a moment in time which would witness her disappearance and spawn a legend.

Whenever a New York skyscraper is built, the public-relations firm whose responsibility it is to attract attention to the new building boasts not of the structure's location, nor its height, nor even its architectural beauty. Instead, the dauntless publicity men and women will steadfastly claim that their building sports the fastest elevators in the world.

And so it was with the World Trade Center, for a while

the tallest, largest building ever erected, two twin towers soaring above the skyline at the foot of the famous island that the Indians sold for the equivalent of the one-way cabfare to Kennedy Airport.

The ride to the 89th floor took but a few ear-popping seconds.

"I'm glad I don't have to do *that* every day," Sacha commented as she disembarked from the elevator. Denis followed closely behind. "This had better not take long," she continued, glancing at her watch. "I've got to be uptown in an hour."

The thick brown carpet cushioned their footsteps as they walked to the plush reception area on the right of the bank of elevators. The name of the firm, Greer, Holmes and Co., was elegantly proclaimed in gold letters above a mahogany doorway. Inside, an elderly male receptionist sat behind a large desk and acknowledged them as they approached.

"May I help you?" the receptionist offered in a voice of distinct upper-crust origins.

"Mr. Jason Caldwell, please," Denis asked. "We were told by your Des Moines office that we would find him here."

"Yes, of course," the man replied while Denis and Sacha traded smiles. Their search was over, and at the thought of the discovery, their excitement mounted. They had found a man who might answer the myriad questions about the ship, its mission, the gold, and, above all, the role of Amelia Earhart in whatever secret mission the *Sherman* had been assigned.

A door behind the reception area opened and a middle-aged woman appeared. The receptionist greeted her with a smile. "Oh, Doris, these people are looking for Mr. Caldwell."

"I'm Denis Keyser," Denis volunteered. "Is Mr. Caldwell in?"

"Well . . . uh, no," the woman replied hesitantly.

"Is he off today?" Denis persisted.

"Actually, he's on a leave of absence," the woman admitted, and Denis noticed a slight smirk on her face. Suddenly his premature sense of accomplishment seemed a distant memory.

"Are you his secretary?" Denis asked.

"No. Jason . . . uh, Mr. Caldwell doesn't have his own secretary, but one of the girls inside helps him out. Are you a client?"

"Not yet. Mr. Caldwell was recommended to me by a mutual friend. May I speak to the young lady you referred to?"

"Certainly," Doris said. "Please follow me."

The trading room bustled with seemingly important activity as Denis and Sacha wended their way through its rows of desks and electronic gadgets on the way to the brokers' area. As they passed by, countless shirtsleeved young men, the professional stock traders, shouted letters and numbers at one another and pushed buttons on colorful consoles built into their desks. Overhead, an illuminated ticker flashed the electronic green stock symbols of the securities traded on the New York Stock Exchange.

The atmosphere among the brokers seemed decidedly more subdued, like a gentlemen's club where business transactions are discussed in hushed tones, if they must be discussed at all. Here the men did not shout, but spoke quietly on the phone, and occasionally pressed buttons on a computer-console-type machine. Doris led them directly to a desk in the rear, where an attractive secretary with long auburn hair pecked at her IBM typewriter.

"Mimi, this is Mr. and Mrs. . . . oh, I'm sorry," Doris said. "I forgot your name."

"Never mind," Denis retorted, "thanks for showing us the way."

Mimi looked up from her typewriter and smiled broadly. "Can I help you?" she said in a bouncy, enthusiastic voice.

"Why, yes," Denis continued, while Sacha surveyed the wide trading area. "I'm trying to locate Jason Caldwell. I understand he's on a leave of absence."

Mimi giggled, then apologized.

Denis gave her one of his winning grins. "Hey, you're the second person who seems to think Jason's leave of absence is pretty funny. What's going on?" His eyes flashed a let-me-in-on-the-secret look.

"I really shouldn't say..." Mimi said tentatively. "Are you a friend of his?"

"Sort of. I'd really like to know what's going on, Mimi. How about it?" The smile was still there in force.

"Well, I mean, it's no secret," Mimi said, fidgeting with her typewriter. "It's just that Jason was so straight! Then we all heard that he and Peggy Allenby took a leave of absence—*together*. If ever there were two people you wouldn't—"

"Peggy Allenby?" Denis interrupted. While pretending not to pay attention, Sacha, whose back was turned, discreetly noted the name on a slip of paper and slid it into her purse.

"Yes, she's an analyst in the Research Department. About twenty-five years younger than Jason, too."

"Hey, that old son-of-a-gun!" Denis said with all the enthusiasm he could muster. "Where did they go?"

"We don't know. Somebody said California."

"Isn't Jason married?"

"No."

"Peggy?"

"No."

"They live together?"

"You're awfully nosy, you know."

Denis resorted to the big smile. "My mother keeps telling me that, too."

Mimi smiled back and held her eyes on Denis' for a brief flirtatious moment. Then she glanced aside and met Sacha's icy stare.

"Do they live in Manhattan?" Denis persisted.

Mimi looked cautiously at Sacha, then turned her attention back to Denis. "They don't live together. Jason lives on the West Side and Peggy lives in Queens, with her mother, I think."

"Thanks, Mimi. I guess I'll just get in touch with Jason when he gets back."

"Could one of the other brokers help?" Mimi offered.

"No, that's okay," Denis said as he and Sacha turned to leave. "My inheritance won't settle for another couple of months. Thanks anyway."

They walked swiftly through the cavernous lobby of the World Trade Center while Sacha scurried to keep pace with Denis' longer stride.

"I can't leave you alone for one goddamn minute," she wailed. "You had that little secretary making goo-goo eyes at you!"

Denis grinned and kept up the quick cadence. "Can I help it if I'm irresistibly charming?" He spotted a bank of telephones against a distant wall and headed for it.

"Let me guess," Sacha said. "You're calling your mother."

"Wrong," Denis said as he dropped a dime in the slot.

"The office?"

"Wrong again. You've got one more guess."

Sacha reached into her purse and pulled out a slip of paper. "Peggy Allenby's mother."

Denis dialed 411. "You knew it all along, didn't you?"

"Yep. And I also know that if you want a number in Queens, you dial 555-1212. Not 411."

L. Allenby, of Rego Park, Queens, answered on the third ring.

"Mrs. Allenby? Hi. This is John Lipton. I'm a friend of Jason Caldwell's. I can't seem to reach him and his office thought you might be able to help."

"Who told you I might help?" said the elderly female voice in a suspicious tone.

"His secretary, ma'am. She was only doing her job."

"Well, they don't want anyone to know their whereabouts."

Denis continued in a cheerful voice. "But I've got some good news, Mrs. Allenby. Jason's come into some money. His uncle Charlie died—Jason probably doesn't even remember him—and he left his nephew a sizable portion of his estate. I'm sure Jason would like to know."

"Oh, that is good news!" the woman exclaimed. "Believe you me, that's the kind of news Jason needs to hear. My daughter, too. I'm not sure they're still there, but the last time I heard from Peggy they were staying at the Holiday Inn in downtown Long Beach in California.

Denis scribbled furiously. "Thanks very much, Mrs. Allenby."

Sacha stretched to see over Denis' shoulder and read the address he had written down. "You're terrific with old ladies," Sacha said. "You ought to stick with them."

The familiar sound of clacking typewriters and a swirl of activity greeted Denis as he crisscrossed the *Press*'s newsroom to get to his desk.

"Hey, Denis!" Buddy Levine, Denis' copyboy friend, shouted. "You've got a visitor waiting for you at the reception."

Denis acknowledged the message with a friendly wave and changed course, veering toward the entrance area.

Peter Sloan, clad in a turtleneck sweater and corduroy suit, smiled at the sight of his younger friend. They shook hands and Denis led the way back to his desk, while Peter ambled along behind, clutching a fat briefcase under his arm.

When they arrived at his work sanctuary, Denis cleared away some of the debris, arranging papers and notes in random stacks.

"How's our book coming?" Denis asked.

"Not bad. I've got quite a bit of new material on Earhart. There are still a few people alive who knew her well."

Denis gazed at the stack of notes in Sloan's briefcase. The sight of all that work made him feel guilty. He had put out little effort so far on his share of the book project. Unless, of course, you counted all the investigative work. It had better count, Denis thought. Finding a *Sherman* survivor had been no picnic.

As if he had read Denis' mind, Sloan asked, "Have you uncovered anything about the *Sherman* yet?"

"As a matter of fact," Denis replied with glee, "I have." He leaned back in his swivel chair and put his feet on the area of the desk he had just cleared off. "I've found a *Sherman* survivor."

"God! Where?" Sloan leaned forward in the uncomfortable straight chair. He assumed that the remainder of their conversation should be discussed discreetly.

"Right here in New York," Denis continued, "but he's slipped through our fingers."

Denis caught Buddy Levine's eye and asked him for two Cokes. Then in considerable detail he recounted to Sloan the story of his and Sacha's tracking down of Jason Caldwell, from the identification of Kinderman in Texas, to Jason Carnoff's file at the VA Hospital in San Francisco, the nurse, Rose Mullen, and finally, in Des Moines, the clinching discovery of Jason Carnoff's new identity as Jason Caldwall. But now, it seemed, Caldwell had fled to the West Coast.

Peter Sloan mulled over the series of events for a few seconds, then asked: "But if Caldwell is gone, why not focus on the other survivor you found? What's his name?"

"Kinderman." The Cokes arrived and Denis took a swig. "I found out from him," he continued, wiping his mouth with the back of his hand, "that only Caldwell, among the survivors, was on deck when the *Sherman* went down. So he's our best chance for finding the link between Earhart and the *Sherman*."

Sloan agreed. "Well, how do we get ahold of Caldwell, then?"

"Let's do it right now." Denis returned his feet to the floor. He reached into his side pocket and produced a scrap of paper. "The Holiday Inn in downtown Long Beach," he read aloud.

While he dialed the information operator, Denis almost wished that Sacha were there to supply the area code from her reservoir of trivial data. How *did* she know all those numbers? He reached an operator and got the information he needed. When the number answered, Denis quickly motioned to Sloan to listen in on the phone at an adjoining, vacant desk.

Denis politely asked the woman on the West Coast for Jason Caldwell.

"He's no longer registered here," she replied in a singsong voice.

"Do you know where I can reach him?"

"No idea, sir."

"Who's the manager there?" Denis asked.

"Pat Roselli. Would you like to speak to him?"

Roselli was on the line in just a few seconds and remembered Jason Caldwell. In fact, the Caldwells had stayed at his inn for over two weeks. Nice folks, too. Just checked out yesterday.

"Is there anything you can tell me that might help me find him, Mr. Roselli? It's quite important."

There was a momentary silence on the California end of the conversation. "Say, who are you, anyway?" Roselli asked.

"My name is John Lipton," Denis continued, resorting to his favorite alias. "I'm an attorney in New York. Mr. Caldwell has inherited some money and I'm trying to locate him."

"Well . . ." the motel manager said, apparently satisfied with the story. "He never really said what business he was in, but I do know that the Caldwells spent a lot of time at the Worldwide Salvage Company, down by the docks."

Denis and Peter Sloan stared at each other and recognized the mutual look of slow shock that overcame their faces. Denis thanked Roselli for the information and hung up.

"Holy shit!" Denis shouted, and before Peter Sloan could put his two cents in, Denis attacked the phone again. He secured the number of the Worldwide Salvage Company and rang them straightaway.

Peter Sloan listened in, his ear glued to the receiver,

while Denis went through his now-familiar routine about Jason Caldwell's inheritance.

"Gee, that's awfully nice," the young voice said upon learning of Jason's good fortune.

"Do you know where I might find him?" Denis asked. His heart nearly stopped as he waited for the reply.

"They left yesterday," she said in a nasal, plaintive tone. "On the *Princess.* Mr. Denton—he's our president—took them on a salvage mission."

"Salvage mission?"

"Yes, sir. To the South Pacific somewhere. But I can get a message to Mr. Caldwell if you wish. They're calling at Honolulu on Tuesday."

"Uh, thanks, miss," Denis stammered, his mind racing, outpacing his words. "That won't be necessary."

Denis kept his hand clutched to the phone when the call was over. He stared at Sloan. "The son of a bitch is after the gold!" Denis shouted.

Sloan, in a mental state approaching shock, stared mutely at Denis. How? Why? his eyes demanded.

"Caldwell must know—or think he knows—where the *Sherman* went down. Since he was the only survivor on deck, that's entirely possible."

Sloan thought about that for a moment. "If that's true," he said, "why did Caldwell wait this long to go find the *Sherman?*"

"Because, my friend, I'll bet a month's pay that before he read my story on the *Sherman,* Mr. Caldwell didn't have the slightest notion that there was a fortune in gold on that ship."

"Of course!" Sloan exclaimed. "And if that Australian woman is really Amelia Earhart, she'll know the ship's location too. So Caldwell has to get there before she reveals it."

"Exactly. In the meantime, my story—and our book— is now sailing away to Honolulu. Which leaves us but one choice."

Denis stood up and gazed across the room to see if

Latelle was in his office. He was—on the telephone, of course.

"I hope you've got an understanding department head at Georgetown," Denis said soberly, "because if we want to salvage our own little project, we'd better get our asses to Honolulu and on that ship!"

part
TWO

chapter
15

Were it not for the nagging pressure of the *Sherman-Earhart* case, which now occupied all of his time, Colonel Stan Cerilla might have spent the weekend batting the hell out of a tennis ball. He played an intense game, in which he vented his weekday frustrations with powerful ground strokes whose force frequently carried the ball well beyond the baseline. Instead, Cerilla spent this sunny Saturday morning in his Pentagon office, along with a full complement of cheerless staffers.

"Here's the file, Colonel." Captain Turner handed Cerilla a manila folder about an inch thick with the words "Top Secret" stamped on its cover in bold letters. "Please sign the receipt down here and I'll take it over to the duty officer."

Cerilla scribbled his name on the security document and took possession of the file.

"Oh, uh, Colonel. I put the security-check report on Keyser in your In basket. It came through last night."

"Thanks, Turner," Cerilla said. "I don't think I'll be needing you anymore today. You might still have time for nine holes."

Turner smiled thankfully, and almost sprinted to the door. "Thank you, Colonel. I'm going to do just that."

When the junior officer had left, Cerilla opened the Earhart file and leafed through the familiar documents. He wondered how many of its pages of investigative data, false leads, erroneous newspaper stories, and solid fact he might have already committed to memory, so often he had pored over this material searching for clues he might have missed before.

Suddenly a familiar voice addressed him from across the office. Turner had returned.

"Turner? I thought you had gone," Cerilla commented.

"There was something I forgot to tell you, sir," the young man said sheepishly.

"What?"

"It may not be anything at all, but when I was down in Classified Documents getting the *Sherman* file, Lieutenant Crowley mentioned that a reporter was asking questions recently about *Sherman* survivors. Somebody called Crowley to find out how tight the lid was on that information."

"Damn." Cerilla grimaced. "I suppose the reporter was Denis Keyser."

"I don't know, and neither does Crowley. The person who called was from upstairs." Turner raised his eyes in reference to the senior military and civilian staffs whose offices were one floor above their own. Smart reporters made friends with various assistant secretaries, then asked the officials to do their dirty work.

"Well, I'm pretty damn sure Keyser is behind this one way or another. That pushy little prick won't let up. And I'll tell you something, Turner," Cerilla continued, his steely eyes fixing the younger officer. "If Keyser manages to break the story of the Earhart-*Sherman* connection and then starts a treasure hunt for the gold, well, I'm afraid that's going to be my ass. We don't want that to happen, do we?"

Turner stiffened to attention. "No, sir!" he barked.

"All right, Captain," Cerilla said with a sigh. "Keep your eyes and ears open and get back to me on any intelligence like the kind you just came in with. That all helps, you understand?"

Turner nodded emphatically but did not leave.

The colonel reached into his In basket and pulled out the report on Denis Keyser. He leafed through the first two pages until, on page three, his eyes caught an unusual item. "I'll be damned," Cerilla muttered.

"Sir?"

"I think we've found a little ammunition, Turner," Cerilla said. He thought for a brief moment, then added: "I'm going to take the shuttle to New York this afternoon. It's about time we took the offensive."

"Who could that be?" Sacha said as she wiped her mouth with the paper napkin. Denis was already up and on his way to the door. He unbolted the two locks and opened to find the tall uniformed gray-haired officer.

"Why, Colonel Cerilla. This *is* an unexpected surprise. Won't you come in?" Denis offered with an exaggerated sense of courtesy.

Cerilla removed his cap and stepped into the cluttered apartment. He acknowledged Sacha, who was seated at the small dining table, where a half-consumed candle flickered from its perch on an empty Chianti bottle. A large white pizza box dominated the tabletop.

"Allow me to introduce," Denis said as he ushered Cerilla into the room. Denis introduced Sacha to Cerilla, and the colonel smiled politely.

"I hope I'm not intruding," Cerilla said, knowing, of course, that he was.

"No problem. How about some pizza? You like pepperoni?" Denis picked up a limp piece and handed it to the colonel."

"No, thanks, Keyser. I've already eaten."

"Well, we haven't finished, Colonel, so why don't you pull up a chair and sit down."

Sacha's eyes darted from one man to the other, waiting for someone to get to the point of this unexpected meeting. Denis poured another glass of wine and chomped at a fresh slice of pizza while Cerilla took a seat and accepted a half glass of wine.

"You just happened to be in the neighborhood, right, Colonel?" Denis said, smiling.

"No . . . I wouldn't say that," Cerilla replied seriously. "I think it's time we came clean with each other on this *Sherman* business."

"Sure, Colonel. You mean I tell you everything I know and you do the same, right?"

"Not exactly."

"Then no deal." Denis took another bite and chewed loudly.

"There are questions of national security involved here," Cerilla continued. "In fact, I can probably prevent you from printing any classified information you obtain surreptitiously."

"Ah, Colonel," Denis said. "Someday you and I should have a long talk about the First Amendment. It's funny how they don't seem to teach that at West Point. Are you sure you don't want some pizza?"

Cerilla shook his head, then spoke to Denis in a quiet but commanding tone. "I understand you've been talking to some people at the Pentagon."

Denis shrugged and continued eating.

"That puts you," Cerilla continued, "in the position of a reporter covering the Defense Department."

"Bully."

"Yes. Quite. But you should know that all journalists who are accredited to the Defense Department must pass a thorough security check beforehand."

"Go on, Colonel," Denis said.

Sacha instantly sensed the anxiety building within Denis. She wondered what game Cerilla was playing.

"There's something in your background," Cerilla went on dispassionately, "that makes you unacceptable for accreditation to the Defense Department. I'm sure you know what I'm talking about."

Denis glowered at Cerilla. Sacha touched Denis' hand but it was cold and unyielding. Denis stood abruptly.

"Get out of here!" he shouted at Cerilla. But the colonel did not move.

"Calm down, Keyser. I want to talk to you, that's all."

Sacha took Denis' arm and tugged gently. Slowly Denis regained control of his emotions and sat down. He pushed the unfinished pizza aside.

"Say what you have to say, Colonel."

"As a matter of policy, the military would prefer not to be covered by someone who has received a dishonorable discharge from the service. I think the reasons are obvious."

"My discharge had nothing to do with my attitude toward the Army!" Denis protested.

"That's your opinion. I did not come to debate the circumstances of your discharge. What I want from you, Keyser, is simple. Stay off the Defense Department beat, and that includes any incidents involving American warships."

"You're blackmailing me, Cerilla."

"I am doing nothing of the kind. I am, however, giving you a warning. A friendly warning. If the Press assigns you to any story involving the Defense Department, we will inform the newspaper in writing of your unacceptability."

Denis lowered his head for a moment before facing Cerilla again. "I want to think it over."

Cerilla nodded and left the table. He picked up his cap and said good-bye to Sacha, apologizing again for having interrupted their evening. Denis didn't bother to look up as the colonel let himself out of the apartment.

Sacha poured the rest of the wine in their glasses, waiting impatiently for Cerilla to be out of earshot. Then she softly asked her question. "Is that true about the dishonorable discharge?"

"Yes, it is," Denis responded, his voice sullen. "I've never told you, but I went into the service right after high school. There was no money for college and I didn't get the basketball scholarship I was hoping for. Then there was the draft to worry about, so I enlisted. I figured I could go to college after the Army on the GI Bill.

"The incident Cerilla alluded to involved a sergeant in basic training. I can still see that bastard's face, just as if he were standing here. I was a smart-aleck city kid, not one of the hillbilly Southern boys he was used to. So he paid special attention to me, like giving me twice as much extra duty as anybody else, and haranguing me in front of the other troops."

"Sounds awful," Sacha commented while she lit a long brown cigarette.

"It gets worse. The sergeant had another little surprise for me. One night, while we were on a three-day field exercise, he came over to where I was sleeping. He woke me up and mumbled something about not having all that extra duty anymore. Then he put his hand on my crotch and told me to take my pants off. Instead, I beat him senseless."

"My God!"

"I was court-martialed, and they didn't believe my story. The sergeant had twenty years of service on his side, and according to him, I disobeyed a lawful order and hit him. I tried to get others to testify to the sergeant's sexual behavior, but no one would. I suspect that he never propositioned more than one guy in each platoon."

"Oh, Denis," Sacha lamented, "don't you think the people at the Press would understand?"

Denis shook his head. "They don't know I was in the service, so they don't know about my discharge. I'll bet Cerilla had someone check my employment application at the paper. He'd have found out that I didn't list any military service. Jesus, Latelle would have a fit if he knew. He's a gung-ho reserve officer."

"Would they fire you?"

Denis sighed. "I don't know, Sacha. Maybe not. But I could forget about getting any decent assignments. I'd be too vulnerable. A dishonorable discharge is serious business."

"What are you going to do?"

"Well, the colonel won't have to worry about my hanging around the Pentagon, because I'm going to Hawaii to track down Caldwell. I'll worry about Cerilla's threat when I get back."

"Good weekend, sir?"

"Not too bad, Captain." Cerilla had returned to Washington with a certain sense of satisfaction on the last shuttle Saturday night, gone to bed, worked out at a nearby Arlington gym on Sunday, and read the Washington *Post*. Your average Cerilla weekend.

"I've got a preliminary report from the Bureau," Turner said cheerfully. He laid the paper on Cerilla's desk.

Cerilla buried himself in the document at once. He had had to invoke national security to get a wiretap rigged to Keyser's phone, the only way he could do it without a court order. At least his friends at the Bureau would not keep a record of the request.

"Well, here's something," Cerilla commented. "Two phone calls from Peter Sloan. I know him—that Georgetown professor who's done some research on Amelia Earhart."

"That's right, sir," Turner acknowledged. "And you'll read a little further down that they're collaborating on a book, a book about the connection between Amelia Earhart and the USS *Sherman*."

"Jesus Christ." Cerilla sighed. "Any information on whether they found any of the *Sherman* survivors?"

"We don't know, sir. They didn't discuss that in the telephone conversations we tapped. But—"

"I think we'd better have them tailed, Captain."

"I was about to say, sir," Turner rejoined, "that the Bureau did that for us. But they both have just left—flew off to Hawaii."

"Hawaii? Why the hell did they go there?" Cerilla thought for a moment, and the incident involving Denis Keyser's court-martial popped into his mind. "You don't think they're queer, do you?"

"No, sir, definitely not. Besides, from what I hear, Keyser's girlfriend is some knockout."

"She is," Cerilla agreed, as his mind wandered back to the brief meeting in Denis' apartment. "Now, let's make sure someone picks up their trail in Hawaii. I want to know what those two are doing there."

"I'll take care of that, Colonel. And shouldn't we notify the Press about Keyser's background?"

"No, not now. I'll use that information when I have to, but this isn't the right time. Let's find out what Keyser's up to first."

"Anything else, sir?"

"Just one more thing, Turner. It's time I had a private word with Mrs. Stenemond. I know those doctors aren't going to like it, but that's just too bad. Find out for me how much that Medical Institute gets in government grants. It never hurts to know where your leverage is."

chapter
16

She wore the same old-fashioned dress as the last time
Cerilla had seen her. Only now she was not hidden behind
a glass partition but seated next to him on a small settee.
Dr. Wilton was also present, and assumed the dual role of
moderator and protector of his patient. With characteristic
grace Mrs. Stenemond smiled and chatted amiably with
Colonel Cerilla about her stay in California. Since her
health was uncertain, there had been few excursions outside the hospital, but those few sorties had been pleasant
and gratifying.

After they had conversed for about ten minutes, Dr.
Wilton concluded that Mrs. Stenemond was relaxed
enough for him to begin inducing a trance. He spoke to her
slowly, repeating certain phrases in a monotonous voice.
Cerilla observed silently as Mrs. Stenemond's eyes became
glassy and her attention drifted away from them. Within
minutes the trance had taken.

Dr. Wilton nodded, Cerilla's cue that he could proceed
with the questioning.

"It's good to see you again, Amelia," Cerilla stated
sincerely. Amelia Earhart had played so important a role
in his professional career that he could scarcely begin to

describe his feelings when in the company of this woman.

"I'm happy to see you again, sir." The voice was stronger than Mrs. Stenemond's had been earlier.

"Amelia," Cerilla began, as he mentally composed his sentence, "I'd like to talk about your last flight. Can we discuss that?"

She did not answer right away. A veil of pain seemed to draw over her face. "I . . . I think so," she replied hesitantly.

"Your last flight took you from Lae to Howland, did it not?"

"Yes."

"Had you agreed to undertake a special mission on that leg of the journey, Amelia? A mission for the government?"

Again she hesitated. "I am sworn to secrecy," she said finally.

Cerilla decided on another tack. "Do you recall anything about a Project Sherman, Amelia?"

"Yes . . . a ship . . . wreckage . . . bodies . . ."

"Where, Amelia? Where did you see all this?" Cerilla could not contain the excitement in his voice.

"The atoll . . . the . . . oh, the noise! The fire! Poor Fred. He was bleeding so! Please . . . Let me go back. I do not wish to stay here. . . ." Suddenly she could no longer speak. Her voice gave way to heavy sobs, and she buried her face in her frail hands.

"I'm afraid that will be all," Dr. Wilton said firmly as he moved over to comfort Mrs. Stenemond. "Clearly she is not ready for this type of questioning."

"When can I continue, Doctor?" Cerilla pleaded. "It's of the utmost importance."

"I'm not sure you ever can, Colonel. It is obviously a painful subject for her. I will have to be the judge of when you can continue. It could be tomorrow, or it could be . . ." Wilton shrugged.

Cerilla glanced at Mrs. Stenemond, who had now regained control of her emotions. She sat serenely, her head lowered. Reluctantly Cerilla realized that he had no alternative but to leave. The mighty Pentagon, with all of its intimidating forces, could exert no pressure on an Australian physician and his elderly patient. The information he needed, if it was indeed buried in the depths of Mrs. Stenemond's mind, would come forth at a time of her own choosing. The mystery of the *Sherman* and Amelia's mission, the gold and its whereabouts, would remain a secret until, like a ticking time bomb, the moment for release arrived.

Cerilla was interrupted at the door as he prepared to leave the Medical Institute. A male orderly ran after him, calling his name.

"There's a phone call from Washington, Colonel. The man says it's important!"

The orderly led the colonel to a small waiting room where he could take the call in relative privacy. Cerilla identified himself and heard Captain Turner's voice on the other end.

"I've got some interesting news, Colonel," Turner reported. "The FBI just got back to us on Keyser and Sloan. Yesterday they boarded a ship called the *Princess*, which was on its way to somewhere in the South Pacific. Nobody knows where for sure." He paused. "The *Princess* is the best salvage ship in the business, sir. It's being skippered by Soapy Denton himself."

"A salvage ship! Goddammit, Turner, they must be after the *Sherman*. But how the hell would they know where to look?"

"I don't know, sir," Turner said helplessly.

"You'd better get word of this to the Secretary, Captain," Cerilla ordered, regaining his composure.

"That won't be necessary, sir. He called down here a little while ago and I told him. He'd like to see you first thing in the morning."

"Another goddamn red-eye," Cerilla lamented under his breath, anticipating the overnight flight to Washington. "Okay, Turner, I'll be there in the morning. There are a couple of things I want you to do before I get there. Track down every detail of that charter. I want to know the names of every goddamn person on that ship. Run all the names by the Bureau. Oh, and also have them checked against the CIA files. Just a computer check, okay? If any lights go on, follow through on those names. See you in the morning."

"You look tired, Colonel," the Secretary said as he invited Cerilla to take a seat on the sofa. The flags behind the massive desk once again reminded the colonel of the importance of this meeting.

"Yes, sir. I just got in an hour ago."

"Well, I think I'm pretty well up-to-date. Captain Turner briefed me in your absence. It seems this situation has moved along faster than we expected."

Thanks to one pesky newspaper reporter, Cerilla thought. "Yes, sir. I wasn't expecting a salvage mission. I don't know how they hope to find the *Sherman*. We don't know where she lies, and as far as we know, no one else does either."

"Well, there must be somebody on board who thinks he can find her."

"I'm checking out everyone on the ship, sir. We've already got the manifest."

The Secretary signaled his approval. "All right, Colonel. I suggest you finish up that part of the work in a hurry, because I've got a special assignment for you." The Secretary drew a breath while Cerilla waited impatiently to hear what was in store for him. "I've ordered a destroyer from Guam to follow the salvage ship—out of sight, of course. I want you to join up with that destroyer."

Cerilla "yes-sirred" obediently.

"I've arranged a special Air Force flight for you from Andrews to Guam," the Secretary continued. "There you'll be taken by helicopter to the ship. Your flight leaves at twenty-one hundred tonight."

"Yes, sir. Understood."

"And, Colonel, an old friend of mine, Admiral Deke

Crossley, will be in command of the destroyer. He was handpicked for this mission. I'd like you to brief him fully as soon as you are on board."

Cerilla nodded while a thousand thoughts ran through his mind. He wondered how Turner was doing on the manifest.

"I suppose that will be all, Colonel," the Secretary said as he rose from the armchair. "Except to wish you the best of luck." They shook hands and Cerilla headed for the door.

"By the way, Colonel," the Secretary added. "The President asked me to convey his wishes for success as well."

Cerilla raced back to his office, pondering the Secretary's last remark: its meaning was not lost on him. The mission he had just been assigned carried with it the burden of responsibility of a direct mandate from the President.

As soon as he burst into his office, Cerilla's secretary told him that Captain Turner wanted to see him the minute he got back. Cerilla checked his watch, calculated that he had about three hours left before he should go home, pack, do mundane things like cancel the paper delivery before leaving. Call a few friends? He smiled. Would they really care that he had gone? In fact, would anyone notice? Cerilla quickly dispelled the thought and focused his attention on Turner, who had come up alongside. They went into Cerilla's office and closed the door.

"What've you got?" Cerilla asked.

Turner unfolded a piece of paper. "Couple of things. Most everybody on the ship checks out, but we've got a few strange ones. One's a stockbroker from New York, Jason Caldwell. We're having trouble getting a backgrounder on him so the FBI's doing a quick search. We should hear from them any minute."

Cerilla checked his watch. "What else, Captain? I'm in a hurry."

"Well, I don't know what to make of this, sir," Turner said. He handed the paper to Cerilla. "I think you might want to have a talk with the CIA people about it."

Cerilla glanced at the paper and let out a slow whistle. "Christ. This could be something. I'd better get out to Langley and see what else they've got. Give them a call, Turner, will you? That'll save ten minutes at the gate."

The telephone on Cerilla's desk buzzed, a call from his secretary. Turner was closer, so he reached over and picked up the receiver. He identified himself, then spent the next few minutes listening.

"Well, I'll be damned," he muttered.

"What is it, Turner?"

"That stockbroker I told you about? Jason Caldwell. Well, it seems he changed his name about forty years ago. His name was originally Carnoff."

"So what?"

"Well, sir," Turner continued, "one of the survivors of the *Sherman*, a seaman, was one Jason Carnoff. It's the same man, according to the Bureau. The agent said that without their new computers they could never have tracked him down so fast."

Cerilla threw his hands up in exasperation, feeling as if events were going too fast, leaving him behind. "Okay, so there's a *Sherman* survivor with them! So what! Our people interviewed every last *Sherman* survivor forty years ago— check the record on that, Turner—and not one of them knew where the *Sherman* went down. Do you hear me, Turner? Not one!"

Captain Turner avoided Cerilla's eyes for a moment, thinking about his superior officer's outburst. Then he looked back at Cerilla, his face serious and composed. "Maybe one of them lied, sir."

A heavy silence hung over the room while both men pondered Captain Turner's simple observation. It was possible that one of them had lied, but how could you speculate intelligently about an event that had occurred forty years earlier?

Cerilla would think about all of these things on the way to the CIA headquarters in Langley, Virginia. Time was running out.

"So long, Captain," Cerilla said as he picked up his brief-case and cap. I'll see you in . . . well, I'll see you when I get back."

Cerilla had been waiting for twenty minutes when a stocky, fortyish Army major entered the stark waiting room. Major Swanson was one of the handful of military officers stationed at the predominantly civilian Central Intelligence Agency.

"Sorry for the delay, Colonel," the major said perfunctorily. "Things have been a bit jammed up."

Cerilla felt his muscles tense. Majors, no matter where they are stationed, do not keep full colonels waiting. "I wouldn't normally mind, Major," Cerilla said in the haughtiest voice of a field-grade commander, "but the Secretary has put a plane at my disposal tonight and my time is limited."

"I'm sorry, Colonel," the major said, stiffening. Both men sat on gray metal straight chairs. Cerilla, as the senior officer, laid the ground rules. "I presume you've been briefed, Major, on why I'm here."

"Up to a point, sir. It has to do with the security checks on the list of people the FBI came up with."

So the major knew very little, Cerilla thought. It was just as well. The military principle of "need-to-know" was very much operative. No matter how high your security clearance, you were told only the minimum necessary to get the job done.

"There was a problem name on the list?"

"Just one, sir." The major removed a single piece of paper from a thin folder and handed it to Cerilla.

Cerilla gave the document a quick read.

"How certain are you that this person is a foreign agent?" Cerilla demanded.

"If we were sure, sir," the major replied wryly, "the individual would be in jail. At this point, we have no evidence, just suspicions based on known contacts, background, and other information. No real hard stuff. though."

145

"Hmmmm." Cerilla stared at the sheet of paper. "Thanks, Major. This will be a big help."

"If we get any more concrete evidence, shall we pass it on to you?"

"Yes. My office will tell you how to reach me. When transmitting any message to me, Major, use only security code B79 slash 12, and request confirmation of the code before you send the message. Understand?"

"Yes, sir."

"Now, if you'll excuse me," Cerilla said, "I've got a plane to catch."

chapter
17

"Peggy?" Jason called as he poked his head out on deck. The sun shone with blinding intensity and there was nothing to absorb its powerful rays but the infinite breadth of the Pacific Ocean around them.

"Over here!" Peggy shouted from the foredeck. She had been leaning against the railing, her head fully scarved to keep her hair from blowing in the strong wind.

Jason walked cautiously forward, his hand gliding along the rail for support. The ship was not swaying too badly this morning. At least, not like it had the last few days, when half the crew thought they would die of seasickness. Peggy had not ventured out of the cabin for two full days until now.

"How are you feeling?" Jason asked. He kissed her on the forehead.

"Better, thanks. At least I feel that staying alive is a viable alternative."

They had been at sea for over a week and the last land they had seen was part of the Hawaiian coastline.

"Where's Denis?" Peggy asked.

"I think he and Peter are working on their book. Recording their impressions, things like that."

"Do you still think it was a good idea to let them come along?"

"Sure. They're paying their own expenses, and frankly, I kind of like the idea of having a book written about us and the expedition."

Peggy frowned. "I dunno. I still think it complicates things."

"Well, look at it this way, my sweet," Jason said as he put his arm around her. "If we had refused to let them come along, Denis would have written a story for his paper telling the world what we were doing. Then we would have had a dozen ships following us, including half of the Seventh Fleet. I think we made the right decision."

"Because they blackmailed you, that's why."

"Peggy, Peggy," Jason lamented. "Why must you always see the seamier side of life? These are just two men after a story, for God's sake."

The wind changed suddenly and the *Princess* began to rock under the pressure of the buffeting waves. The bow rose, then came down with a thud. Jason and Peggy held on to the railing with both hands.

"Here we go again," Peggy wailed.

"Look!" Jason yelled, pointing to the horizon. "Land!"

"Oh, for Chrissake, Jason. You sound like fucking Christopher Columbus."

Jason lowered his arm and looked disapprovingly at her. "Must you talk that way?"

While Jason and Peggy glowered at each other, Soapy Denton came up to where they were standing. He wore a windbreaker, Levi's, and his crumpled captain's cap.

"You see it?" Soapy asked, motioning in the direction of the land. "That's the Marshall Islands, my friends. We're just about there."

"Thank God for small favors," Peggy muttered.

While the landmass on the horizon occupied their attention, two young crew members came running toward them.

"Captain Denton!" one of the sailors shouted. He was in his mid-twenties and had a full beard on his youthful face. "It's Garvey, sir! He's had an attack of some sort. Right now he's doubled over with pain."

"Christ," Denton mumbled. "Where's Kualchek?"

"Who's Kualchek?" Peggy asked.

"One of the divers, ma'am," the other sailor obliged. "He's had two years of medical school."

"Terrific," Peggy commented with typical sarcasm. "Just what we need in a medical emergency."

Soapy Denton and the two crewmen disappeared in a hurry, leaving Jason and Peggy alone again. They were about to go inside when they saw Denis Keyser walking toward them. He wore stylish jeans and a long-sleeved shirt. His face was Riviera tan and healthy-looking.

"What's going on in there?" Jason inquired.

"I think the kid's had an attack of appendicitis," Denis said as he moved up beside them on the railing.

"Can they do anything for him?" Peggy asked.

Denis shrugged. "Kualchek observed an appendix operation once when he was in medical school. That makes him the ship's surgeon, if necessary."

"Je-sus," Peggy howled.

Suddenly a loud, piercing male scream permeated the air, sending a chill through the group on the deck.

Denis grimaced and turned his head toward the sea. "Try not to think about it," he said in a pained voice. "There's nothing we can do."

"How far away are we from the Pingelap atoll?" Peggy asked, changing the subject.

Denis gazed at the landmass ahead of them and turned to his companions. "They say we ought to be there by morning. I guess, Jason, you ought to be fine-tuning your recollections of island imagery."

The Navy helicopter sputtered and landed on the white cross painted for that purpose on the deck of the destroyer. Colonel Cerilla, holding his cap against the rotor blades' windblast, disembarked briskly and was ushered into the ship's interior. Within minutes he was seated in Rear Admiral Deke Crossley's stateroom. The admiral, a perfect John Wayne specimen of the salty naval officer, had distinguished himself many times in his forty-year naval career, including special commendations for heroism during the battle of Midway. Crossley greeted Cerilla with appropriate military courtesy and invited him to take a seat.

"Some coffee, Colonel?"

Cerilla accepted the offer and Crossley nodded to his orderly.

"Well, it seems we've got quite a mission on our hands," Crossley said in a slow, gravelly voice.

"Yes, sir," Cerilla replied with a half smile. "It's different, all right."

They chatted briefly about the ship and its base. Cerilla learned that the destroyer had been at sea for several days and that their present position was northeast of the Marshall Islands.

Crossley continued with the briefing on their location. "We had to pass the Marshalls to the north to pick up the track of the *Princess*. We are now about a hundred and twenty miles behind her and closing in."

"We can track the *Princess* that accurately?" Cerilla said with a note of surprise in his voice.

Crossley laughed. "We do it by satellite now. Here, let me show you." Crossley leaned his hulk over the table and picked up a folder containing some graph paper that had obviously been inscribed by some kind of computer printout device. The graph showed the contours of several islands and the location of what was apparently two ships. "See," Crossley demonstrated, pointing at one of the ships with a pencil. "That's us. And this over here is the *Princess*. We know exactly where they are, but of course, at this distance they have no idea they're being followed. I get this updated every half hour." Crossley moved the pencil over to a group of islands just forward of the other ship's location on the graphic display. "And my guess is that this is where they're heading. Somewhere in the Marshalls. By tomorrow afternoon we should be as close to them as we want to get."

Cerilla nodded faintly. "Before then, Admiral, I should brief you on the details of the mission."

"I'm looking forward to that, Colonel. I'm especially interested in hearing about Amelia Earhart. I was a big fan of hers, you know. I followed all her flights when I was a kid."

"Would you like me to begin now, sir?" Cerilla said, hoping the admiral would not accept. Cerilla had flown nearly halfway around the world and had not slept in a proper bed for two days.

"No, save it, Colonel. I'm sure you're tired, so I'm going to let you rest. I want a first-class briefing, and I don't think you're in any shape to give me one now."

Cerilla wasn't going to argue. The rest, no matter how brief, would be welcome.

"My orderly will show you to your quarters," Crossley continued. "You'll be awakened in five hours."

The small group of people crowded together around the mess table in the stateroom. Although there was occasional sporadic conversation, no one ever found a subject worthy of sustained discussion. They all knew that the most pressing order of business was the medical operation going on next door. Jason and Peggy held hands, Denis sat quietly, and Peter Sloan took long, slow puffs on his pipe, filling the room with billows of sweet-smelling smoke.

Suddenly Soapy Denton burst in on them. "The kid's going to make it," he announced. A cathartic spell of relief permeated the room while everyone breathed audible sighs.

"Thank God," Peggy intoned.

Denton grinned broadly and lit up a cigar, soon to add to the foul air in the stuffy stateroom. "Garvey won't be of any use to us diving, but at least he's going to be all right. That Kualchek would've made one helluva fine surgeon."

A bottle of scotch found its way to the table and an instant party sprang to life, replete with jubilation. When the moment had passed, Soapy Denton took Jason aside and spoke to him quietly.

"I estimate the Pingelap atoll within twenty-four hours," Soapy said. "Are you sure you're going to remember where that ship went down?"

Jason took a sip from the glass he was holding. "If you can orient this boat in the right direction, I know I'll find it. I know just what to look for."

"Colonel Cerilla." A male voice called his name and a firm hand shook him at the shoulder.

"Hunhh," Cerilla mumbled, opening his eyes slowly. The faint light stung his eyes, so he closed them again.

"There's an urgent phone call for you. From the Pentagon."

"Okay, okay," Cerilla said, waking slowly. He put a robe around his naked body and followed the orderly through the ship.

They reached the communications shack and Cerilla picked up the phone. Turner was on the line.

"For Christ's sake, Captain, couldn't you let me have a couple hours' sleep?"

"'Fraid not, sir," Turner said, not sounding the least bit contrite. "We've got a new problem."

"Let's hear it."

"Our friends at the New York *Daily Press* have been pushing hard for an interview with Mrs. Stenemond. They seem hell-bent on proving that their story about the *Sherman* was right."

"Listen, dammit. Tell those people at the Institute that there should be no interviews. Not until—"

"I did that, sir," Turner rejoined dryly. "The executive director got huffy and said that he does not take orders from the Pentagon. With Dr. Wilton's accord, he not only authorized an interview, he made it a full press conference so he wouldn't have to worry about being bombarded by requests from the other papers."

"That's swell, Turner," Cerilla said sarcastically.

"Should I try talking to the Press, sir? Maybe we can persuade them to—"

"No. No. Forget that. Every time you talk to one of those newspaper people they go into a tirade about the First Amendment."

"I could tell them about Keyser, sir," Turner persisted.

"Save it. That won't do us any good now. He's out of touch—on that salvage ship."

"Well, what shall I do then, Colonel?"

Cerilla did not reply.

"Sir? Did you hear me?" Turner asked.

"Yes. I heard you, Turner. I was thinking. You know, I'm not sure that press conference would be so harmful to us. When is it?"

"Tomorrow afternoon."

"All right. I don't want to go into it now, but get word to the Secretary that if my hunch is right, we don't have to worry about Mrs. Stenemond telling anybody where the *Sherman* is. Got that?"

"Uh, yes, Colonel. But, if I may ask, sir, what if you're wrong?"

"Let's cross that bridge when we get to it. You be at that press conference, Captain. And get back to me right afterward."

When they had hung up, Cerilla turned to the orderly and asked how much time he still had to sleep before his meeting with Admiral Crossley. Two hours, was the answer.

"I'll take every minute I can get," Cerilla mumbled, and dragged himself back to his quarters.

chapter
18

Weeks before the announcement of the press conference, the story of Amelia Earhart and Mrs. Emily Stenemond had gradually drifted to the back pages of newspapers, then out of print altogether. The stories died not from lack of interest but from a dearth of information about the affair. There was simply nothing new to report. Nothing, that is, until the press conference was announced, and once again Amelia was back on page one.

The ground rules for the press conference were set forth in the Medical Institute's own release: two journalists would be permitted to ask direct questions of Mrs. Stenemond, under the supervision and guidance of her personal physician, Dr. James C. Wilton. Other reporters and accredited members of the media would monitor the proceedings over a voice hookup in the Institute's auditorium. No other live radio or television coverage would be allowed. The Miami *Herald* later reported that it learned that one network had offered the Institute a half million dollars for exclusive television-coverage rights. The Institute's executive director flatly refused. Another newspaper report suggested that Mrs. Stenemond's physician had accepted a large sum of money for his exclusive story about Mrs. Stenemond's claims. Dr. Wilton was not available for comment.

On the day of the interview, every seat in the auditorium was occupied a full hour before the event was to begin. A mob of grumbling reporters who arrived too late to get seats was hastily accommodated on folding chairs in the hallways. The Institute's executive director prayed that a fire inspector would not show up, since the overcrowding would have yielded a half dozen citations.

At precisely three P.M. Emily Stenemond and James Wilton entered the small sitting room where Richard Townsend of the Chicago Tribune and Nancy Carlotti of Newsday were already seated, waiting. Several stand-up microphones were strategically located around the room. The two journalists had been selected by their colleagues through some sort of ritual, the details of which were kept secret from those outside the field of journalism, who would not have understood it anyway.

Mrs. Stenemond smiled and shook hands with the reporters.

"I hope whatever I have to say will justify all the attention," she commented solicitously.

When the subject appeared comfortable, Dr. Wilton induced the trance. He asked the preliminary questions himself. Can you hear me? Yes. Are you comfortable? Quite. Thank you. Are you Amelia Earhart? Yes.

Nancy Carlotti was allowed to ask the first question. She was a comely young woman who wore wire-rimmed glasses to make her appear less attractive than she actually was. Today she was clad in a conservative tailored suit. She consulted her notes and spoke up in a businesslike voice.

"Miss Earhart, we've all been fascinated by your claims these past few weeks, but so far you haven't really touched on the subject that interests us the most—what happened to you on that last flight in July 1937?"

In the auditorium, the packed house quieted down and listened over the loudspeakers. In the back row, dressed in civilian clothes, Captain John Turner took notes, pretending to be a member of the press.

Nancy Carlotti glanced at her notes again for a brief moment. "There have been numerous theories, Miss Earhart, on how you were lost. Some say you simply could not find Howland Island and vanished into the sea; others have suggested you were shot down by the Japanese; and one author, Fred Goerner, has claimed that you were taken prisoner on Saipan."

In the auditorium the restless crowd stirred. "Goddammit, Nancy, you're not there to make a speech!"

"Can you tell us what really happened?" Nancy finally asked.

Mrs. Stenemond began to speak, but her voice produced only meaningless sounds. It seemed as if she didn't know where to begin. Dick Townsend, the Chicago *Tribune* man, leaned over and whispered something into Carlotti's ear. She agreed, and spoke again.

"Uh, Mrs. Stenemond, would it be easier if I just asked you direct questions?"

Mrs. Stenemond nodded, and Dr. Wilton also signaled his approval.

"All right, then. One of the last messages received by the cutter *Itasca*, which was monitoring your flight off Howland Island, was that you were on a line of position of 157 dash 337, running north and south. Were you lost at that point?"

"Yes."

"What happened to you in the hours that followed that message?"

Mrs. Stenemond paused before replying. "Fred and I circled in a wide arc, transmitting over our assigned frequencies of 6210 and 3105 kilocycles. We were running low on fuel. Finally we found a small atoll and I crash-landed near the beach. Fred was hurt when we landed and he was bleeding. . . . There was broken glass all around and . . ." Mrs. Stenemond's voice cracked slightly. Dr. Wilton motioned to Nancy Carlotti not to resume the questioning for a few seconds.

When Mrs. Stenemond appeared to have regained composure, Nancy asked her to continue.

"We waded ashore. There were some natives. We carried Fred to a hut."

The auditorium group stirred. As most of the reporters knew, the account so far matched a theory advanced by Fred Goerner in his 1966 book, *The Search for Amelia Earhart*. He claimed that after their capture, Earhart and Noonan were taken to the Japanese headquarters on Saipan and later executed because, Goerner alleged, they had been on a secret mission to survey possible Japanese fortifications of the mandated islands. Goerner's book, however, made no mention of Project Sherman.

As originally agreed, the two reporters would alternate their questioning twice at ten-minute intervals for a total interview time of forty minutes, the maximum allowed by Dr. Wilton. Now Dick Townsend prepared to take over. He was an affable man in his early thirties and his colleagues expected that, if anything, Dick could charm the answers out of the old woman.

"I truly hope this session isn't painful to you, Miss Earhart," Townsend began, "but, as I know you realize, your answers may well clarify a mystery that has puzzled the world for forty years."

"I understand the importance, sir."

"Well, then, Miss Earhart. In the original press conference, Dr. Wilton here claimed that you referred to a Project Sherman. Now, no one has been able to learn what that might refer to. One of our colleagues, a reporter in New York, who unfortunately could not be here today, published a story that the *Sherman* was an American ship loaded with gold and that there may have been some connection between it and your disappearance. Is this so?"

Mrs. Stenemond coughed nervously.

"Perhaps my question was too long, Miss Earhart?" Townsend offered in a concerned tone.

"No, sir. I understood your question fully. That is not the problem."

"May I ask what is the problem?"

"Well, you see, sir, certain aspects of my flight were classified. I took an oath not to reveal them to anyone, and I am not prepared to break my oath now."

"But that was forty years ago!" Townsend protested.

Mrs. Stenemond's voice was full of serious intent. "Perhaps. But my oath was forever."

Townsend, perplexed, huddled with Nancy Carlotti and Dr. Wilton, then resumed his interrogation.

"Miss Earhart, Miss Carlotti has just informed me that the United States Department of the Navy, under the directives of the Secretary of Defense, has stated publicly that all information relative to your flight was fully declassified. The declassification occurred in 1967, over ten years ago. So none of the details of your flight are considered a secret anymore. Hence you are no longer bound by your oath."

Mrs. Stenemond squirmed slightly in her chair. "I hope you will take no offense, sir, but I am not prepared to take your word on that."

"All right," Townsend continued, "I take no offense. I understand and respect your allegiance to your oath. But, Miss Earhart, what if I can prove to you that all the facts relating to your flight have been declassified by the United States government? Would you then be prepared to answer my questions?"

"What sort of proof would you offer, sir?"

"I'm thinking about a letter I will request from the Secretary of Defense—he was called the Secretary of War in your day—a letter confirming what I have told you about the declassification. I will see to it that your own physician will be in a position to confirm the authenticity of the letter."

Mrs. Stenemond thought about that for a moment. "Yes," she replied finally. "I will accept that as proof."

Dr. Wilton spoke up. "Since this development will require another session with Mrs. Stenemond, I propose we cut this one short. Are you agreeable?"

Both reporters concurred.

"Another session?" Mrs. Stenemond's voice was strained. "But, Doctor, you told me . . ."

Dr. Wilton took his patient's hand and knelt alongside her chair. He whispered to her for a few moments, and when he had finished, the old woman seemed relaxed.

At a distance, a shuffle of reporters filed out of the auditorium. Only one man remained in place, his eyes glued to his notes. But then Captain Turner had no story to file, no deadline to meet. His report would be read by only one man, the Secretary of Defense, and the Secretary would not like what he read. Not one bit.

The microphones in the sitting room were still on while Mrs. Stenemond shook hands cordially with her two interrogators. She was still in a trance when Nancy Carlotti asked an impulsive question.

"If there was such a ship as the USS *Sherman*, sunk somewhere in the Pacific, would you know where to find it?"

Captain Turner nearly stood at attention as the voice reverberated in the near-empty auditorium.

Mrs. Stenemond was only slightly taken aback by the unexpected question. "Yes, I'm quite sure I could find it," she replied.

As the two reporters walked down the corridor to rejoin their colleagues and fill them in on the background stuff— what she was wearing, facial expressions, and things like that—Nancy touched Dick's arm.

"How long will it take to get the letter?" she asked.

"No more than a week," he replied.

Captain Turner felt totally out of place, a perfectly normal reaction for a junior officer in the presence of the Secretary of Defense. The Secretary, with customary grace, tried to relieve Turner's nervousness.

"How was the flight, Captain?"

"Uh, fine, sir. I slept most of the way."

"Well, I saw the morning papers. That was some show at the Institute."

Turner swallowed hard. "Yes, sir. A real show. But now we have a problem, sir." Turner wished that Cerilla could be there, explaining the options to the Secretary in his usual self-confident manner. Turner was having a hard time just getting the words out.

"I'm the one with a problem, Captain," the Secretary said. He sat behind his massive desk while the young officer stood before him. "From what I read in the papers, I'm expected to produce a letter confirming that all the Amelia Earhart files were declassified in 1967."

"That's right, sir."

"How the hell did that come about?"

"Well, at the press briefing following the interview, Dick Townsend—the Chicago *Tribune* reporter—said that if he got the letter from you confirming the declassification order, Mrs. Stenemond would talk about her mission."

"And the *Sherman?*"

"Nancy Carlotti asked the woman about the *Sherman* as she was leaving the interview. Mrs. Stenemond said she knew where the ship went down."

"I thought she wasn't going to talk about classified information?"

"I think the question caught her by surprise, sir. After all, she is almost eighty years old."

"Well. This is a devil of a situation, Turner," the Secretary commented. "I'm expected to write a letter confirming that all of the Earhart information was declassified when I know damn well that you fellows have a drawer full of top-secret files on her mission. What am I supposed to do, lie about that?"

Turner thought for a moment, then decided that the question was best left rhetorical.

The Secretary spoke on, a tenseness in his voice. "Who was Secretary in 1967? McNamara, wasn't it? Did he really let someone say that all the Earhart stuff was declassified? Didn't he know about Project Sherman?"

"I don't know if he did, sir," Turner said meekly. "Apparently all the Earhart files, except the *Sherman* data, were with Naval Intelligence at the Navy Yard. The Navy closed the file out and declassified it on June 9, 1967."

The Secretary went on. "I don't have much time to decide what to do. If I write that letter, Amelia Earhart could then prove that the government withheld information about her mission and start a fresh scramble for the gold. That's assuming that other group hasn't found it already. If I refuse to give them the letter, I'll be admitting that the government lied back in 1967 when we said that all the information about her flight was declassified. I can't win!"

Turner stood uncomfortably, not uttering a word.

The Secretary gathered some documents on his desk and rose. "Captain, I've got a National Security Council meeting now. When I'm through, I want to get Cerilla on the phone. Start making arrangements for the voice patch to the destroyer. I'll be back in two hours."

chapter
19

"He refused?" Dr. Martin still could not believe what his colleague, Dr. Lash, had just told him. They were both standing in Lash's office at the Institute. The two men wore identical white smocks.

Dr. Lash nodded slowly. "I'm afraid so. Wilton said he did not want you or anyone else talking to his patient when he was not present."

"Well, that sounds pretty damn suspicious to me," Martin said.

"I think you've got to consider his side of this, Lou," Lash rejoined. "Wilton knows you're antagonistic toward him and he doesn't want his patient to get involved."

"Baloney. He's in this for the money."

Lash shrugged. "There's nothing immoral or unethical about his getting paid for a story."

"Unless he's detaining his patient against her will."

"We're going around in circles, Lou."

"Perhaps," Martin conceded. "Perhaps."

Dr. Martin left his colleague in his office, checked his watch, and proceeded to the ward to make his rounds. As he walked past the Institute's wide entrance area, he caught a glimpse of Dr. Wilton dashing out the front door, a small case in his hand.

Martin watched the Australian physician walk through the parking lot until he reached the third row. There, Wilton got into his rented car and drove away.

Martin's pulse quickened. He went straight to the registration desk and spoke to the nurse on duty.

"Where is Mrs. Stenemond staying?" Martin asked.

"We're not supposed to say, Dr. Martin. But I guess it's all right to tell you. She's in Ward 8. Room 6A."

"Thank you," Martin said, and he walked away. A twenty-two-year association with the Medical Institute did have its advantages, he concluded.

Minutes later Dr. Louis Martin alighted on the eighth floor and proceeded directly to 6A. A resident was coming out of the room as Martin went in. Martin didn't recognize the younger doctor, which was just as well.

Mrs. Stenemond was sitting in an armchair gazing out the window at a scene of low, square houses and tree-lined streets. She was fully dressed and turned to see her visitor.

"Mrs. Stenemond? I'm Dr. Martin."

"Yes," she replied. "Won't you sit down."

Martin sat on the edge of the hospital bed. "Mrs. Stenemond, I'm not an expert on hypnosis so I don't know how much you know about why you are here."

The old woman smiled. "I believe that I am Amelia Earhart," she said, "but the recollection of my earlier life only comes to me under hypnosis. I am told that the memories have been suppressed for various reasons which I do not understand."

"I don't have much time," Dr. Martin said, glancing at the door. "What I want to know, ma'am, is if you feel you are being detained here against your will."

"Oh, I have no specific complaints, Doctor. Everyone here has been so kind to me and the food is quite good, really." She paused and her fingers toyed nervously with her long skirt. Then tears began to flow from her eyes as she broke into a muffled sob. "It's true. I do want to go.

... But Dr. Wilton insists that I stay to prove who I really am. I know who I am, Doctor. I don't care what others think."

Martin leaned over to comfort her. He feared she might be on the verge of a breakdown. "Do you wish to return to Australia?" he whispered.

"I just want peace. Anywhere. Someplace where I can live out my last years quietly. Perhaps a small garden. I even have the money ..." Her eyes drifted to the other side of the room, where an old leather purse was resting on the dresser. Then she reached toward Martin with a frail hand and touched his sleeve. "Would you help me? Please, Doctor."

"Yes, I will," Martin said with resolve. He patted her hand, then headed toward the door. "It's best you not talk of our meeting."

The old woman nodded.

"Amelia," Dr. Martin said, using that name for the first time, "my wife and I have always admired you. She's a pilot too, you know. She even met you once when she was a little girl, and she still talks about it."

"Please help me leave here," Mrs. Stenemond said, as Dr. Martin opened the door and quietly departed.

A small group gathered on the windy deck of the *Princess* while the ship cut smoothly through the calm Pacific water. The sun shone as relentlessly as before.

"That's her up ahead," Soapy Denton announced. He pointed to a lumpy landmass on the horizon. "That's Pingelap atoll."

Jason squinted, taking in the first sight of an island he had seen only once before, forty years earlier. "Are you sure?"

Soapy flashed a toothy grin. "Of course I'm sure! We're going to approach the atoll to the northwest. I figure that's the only way the *Sherman* would have passed her, so the scenery should start looking familiar to you."

Perhaps, Jason thought. But it didn't.

Peter Sloan puffed on a pipe and agreed with Denton's strategy. "Is the atoll inhabited?" he asked.

"I doubt it," Soapy replied. "But you can't tell out here. May be a tribe of cannibals on it for all I know."

Jason looked around. "Where's Denis?"

"Listening to the shortwave radio," Peter said, taking a long futile drag on his pipe, which the wind had extinguished. "It's a trait with newsmen. They have a compulsive desire to know what's going on at all times."

The midship doorway clanged open and Denis came out briskly, joining the group. He was clearly upset by something. "She's held a press conference!" he shouted.

"Whoa! Who held what!" Denton asked.

"Amelia just held a press conference and talked about her last flight. They reported it on the Armed Forces Radio news broadcast. She intimated she knew about the *Sherman*, and where it went down."

Sloan looked worried. "Did she say where?"

"No. Apparently she wants clearance from the Defense Department to reveal any other details. The reporters promised to get it for her in a few days."

"We'd better hurry up and stake our claim," Denton commented.

Jason nodded. "Just get the ship to the atoll. I'll take it from there."

"Goddammit," Denis cursed.

Sloan touched Denis' shoulder. "What's the problem? We'll be at the atoll in an hour. We'll be way ahead of everybody else, assuming Jason finds the spot."

"I know that," Denis said, annoyed. "I'm just pissed off about the press conference. I should've been there. This is my story."

"There's a bigger story out here, Denis," Sloan said reassuringly.

Denis nudged Denton, who was gazing at the growing shape of the atoll in the distance. "Say, Soapy, is there any way we can get a telephone hookup to the States over the ship's radio?"

"This is a salvage ship, not the fucking Q.E. Two."

Denton turned his attention back to the horizon. The ship swayed gently as it cut smoothly through the mild blue water.

Now Peggy Allenby joined the on-deck group, clad in blue jeans and a thin sweater. She walked slowly and her eyes were bloodshot.

" 'Morning, everybody," she said with a wave.

"I'm surprised you got up at all," Denton commented sarcastically.

"Up yours, Soapy," Peggy retorted. She put her arm through Jason's and held tight.

"Well, if some of us keep drinking whiskey at the same rate as last night," Soapy added, with an accusatory glance at Peggy, "it's gonna be a pretty dry ride home."

Denis interjected himself in the exchange. "Knock it off, Soapy. Okay? We've all got enough to worry about."

Denis watched Peggy cling affectionately to Jason, while he kissed her forehead. Peggy's hair fluttered in the sea breeze. The scene reminded Denis—although reminders weren't necessary—of how much he missed Sacha. At least if he could talk to her, hear her voice, know what she was doing. But his isolation was total. Often at night, while Peter Sloan rambled on about some professorial subject in the cabin they shared, Denis wished that his roommate would shut up and leave him to his thoughts of Sacha and his fantasies about their being together again.

The atoll grew larger and now all eyes were fixed on the deep green hulk of land jutting out of the Pacific Ocean. A dozen men, crew members and divers, joined the group on deck, sharing the dramatic moment that was soon to take place, the moment when Jason identified the location of the wreck of the Sherman.

"Well?" Denton asked Jason as they approached within three miles of the atoll. At this distance, high hills were clearly visible, a green, lush, rolling panorama.

Jason stared at the atoll, comparing what he saw with a mental photograph indelibly etched in his mind: the hilly shape of a dinosaur. "No . . . it's not right. Maybe when we get closer."

Within minutes the ship had advanced to just over a mile off Pingelap atoll and Soapy ordered the vessel stopped in the water. The *Princess* pitched slightly. Ahead, the green vegetation led down to an inviting sandy beach, where waves broke into sudsy whitecaps and retreated into the ocean.

A thin stream of sweat trickled down Jason's forehead. All eyes were on him now. He followed the shape of the island from shore to shore, trying to remember, trying to see the shape of the dinosaur. But to no avail. "I'm sorry," Jason said. "This isn't the place. Perhaps if we sailed parallel to the island for a while."

Denton gave the order, and the engines started up. They advanced slowly, making no more than ten knots. There were no sounds, save for the breeze and the purring engines.

Jason was concerned now. He leaned against the railing with Peggy still snuggled at his side. Denis stood silently nearby. As the ship moved along, the configuration of the hills changed slightly. But not enough.

Denton paced the deck nervously, chewing on the end of a fat cigar. "Well, goddammit!" he bellowed. "That's the whole fucking island, Caldwell!"

Jason was sweating profusely now. His voice was choked. "It's . . . it's not it. I don't see the dinosaur."

"How long ago did you see that travelogue?" Soapy asked, recalling the story Jason had told him soon after they met.

"It was 1940, I think."

"Well, maybe your fuckin' memory ain't too good!"

"Oh, shut up, you big asshole!" Peggy yelled.

"Sure, lady," Soapy said, calming down. "I hope you've enjoyed your two-hundred-and-fifty-thousand-dollar cruise." He turned and stormed off the deck.

Denis moved a little closer to Jason, whose face suddenly looked older than his years.

"Could it be any other island?" Denis asked. "Something in the vicinity?"

Jason shook his head. "I just don't know anymore. I just don't know."

Denis left the couple to console each other while he went searching for Soapy Denton. He found him in his stateroom.

The captain scowled at his visitor. "What do you want?"

"Let's talk."

"You talk."

Denis found a chair and sat down. "How about looking around the other islands as long as we're out here?"

"Do you have any idea how many islands there are in the South Pacific? Unless you know where you're going, it's hopeless."

"Okay, Soapy. So what will we do?"

"I've already given the order. We're circling around the island and going home. I'm not wasting any more time out here."

"Colonel Cerilla?" The sailor found Cerilla at the small desk in his cabin. He was writing up notes of the earlier briefing he had given Admiral Crossley.

"Yes, come in," Cerilla said loudly. He was unsure of the Navy enlisted man's rank, and that fact embarrassed him. "What is it?"

"There's a message for you from the CIA, sir. But before they transmit, they say you are to confirm the code to be used."

"Tell them B79 slash 12."

"Yes, sir."

In the destroyer's communications center, a technician who was cleared for top-secret material entered the code designation into a small computer. The typewriter console then replied with the word "Accepted."

The technician typed the word "Transmit," and within seconds the typewriter clacked away, translating the coded information into ordinary English, at a speed far surpassing the ability of a human typist.

When the transmission was over, the technician tore off

the single copy of typed paper and placed it in an envelope marked "Top Secret." He then personally delivered the message to Colonel Cerilla.

Alone in his cabin, Cerilla tore the envelope open and read the message.

"Just what I thought . . ." Cerilla said under his breath. "Just what I thought."

A knock on the door interrupted Cerilla's concentration.

"Another message, sir," the sailor announced. "This one's not coded. The Secretary of Defense has ordered a voice patch set up to speak with you and Admiral Crossley, sir. The communication will be ninety minutes from now."

"Fine, sailor. I'll be ready."

While he spoke, Cerilla subconsciously clutched the message he had just received.

"It's all right, Jason. Don't worry." Peggy put her arm around him, comforting him as best she could. They were alone on deck now. The wind had shifted and was cool on their skin.

"All right?" Jason exclaimed. "Peggy, we've just lost a quarter million dollars, we've probably lost our jobs, too, and the SEC may be hot on our trail for the options scheme, for all I know." Jason sighed. "That's what you get for hanging around a loser."

"No, Jason. You're not a loser, dammit. You're not."

"Yes I am, Peggy. I'm one of those people who can't cope with success. Maybe that's why I've always run away from it. I only wish I'd stayed true to form. I don't care about myself, but I got you into this . . ."

"Forget it, Jason." Peggy grasped his shoulders and met his eyes square-on. "I hated my job. I hated everything about what I was doing. But I care about you."

"And, my dear, I let you down, like I always do."

"Oh, Jason, what am I going to do with you?"

As she put her arms around Jason and hugged him, Peggy saw Denis venture out on deck. He waved at them from a distance, not wanting to intrude. Peggy waved back.

"It's okay," she said, and Denis walked over toward them. "What ever happened to that atoll?" she asked.

"It's on the other side of the ship," Denis said, moving up alongside them. "We're circling around the back side on our way home."

Jason said nothing. He walked away slowly, moving around the deck, until he disappeared from view.

Suddenly a loud piercing scream tore through the relative quiet.

Peggy sobbed: "Oh, no!"

Denis, followed frantically by Peggy, ran in the direction of the scream, their feet clacking on the wooden deck. They found Jason on the other side of the ship, leaning against the railing, a strange grin on his face.

"Jason, what is it?" Peggy asked with great concern.

Jason just laughed and pointed over his shoulder.

"He's cracking up!" Peggy exclaimed.

Denis and Peggy took their eyes off him and gazed at the island in the distance, the back side of Pingelap atoll.

There, in front of them, the hills of Pingelap formed the unmistakable shape of a dinosaur.

"Wow!" Denis shouted. And soon the three were embracing one another.

Jason laughed hysterically. "The *Sherman* skipper must have taken her around the back of the atoll for some reason," Jason sputtered. "He may have been trying to avoid a Japanese sub. I don't really care, though. We found it!"

Soapy Denton and Peter Sloan came running out on deck, attracted by the commotion. No one spoke to them, but no one needed to.

Denton looked at the atoll, and its obvious shape, and simply said: "Well, I'll be goddamned."

chapter
20

The *Princess* lay silently in the water, her engines still, her occupants asleep. A quarter moon shone above, outlining the dark silhouette of the ship and its gear. A single sleepy sailor stood watch, checking the time at frequent intervals. It was now two A.M.

Suddenly a grating noise broke the deadly calm. The young sailor quickly opened his eyes and listened attentively. He heard the grating noise again. One of the ship's three motorized tenders was being lowered from its winch. It was probably the portside tender, he thought, but why?

Deliberately the young man rose and headed around the deck, his heavy M1 rifle at his side. At the site of the winch, the sailor looked over the railing and saw a darkly clad figure in the boat unhitching the chains that had lowered him and the tender to the water.

"Halt!" the sailor shouted.

The man in the small boat looked up at the ship and instantly spotted the sailor, whose white uniform stood out against the black background. It also made a good target.

"Who goes there?" the sailor shouted from the railing.

The man in dark clothes below did not respond. He put down the small satchel he was carrying. Then he raised his right arm in a deliberate motion and aimed a .44-caliber pistol at the white target. He fired one muffled shot that whooshed into the sailor's chest. The young man, who had started to raise his rifle, gasped and collapsed onto the railing. As he fell, he fired off a piercing shot from the M1.

At the sound of the shot, lights went on all over the *Princess* and several persons ran out on deck. One of them was Denis Keyser.

"What's going on?" Denis shouted.

A sailor rushed to the side of his fallen colleague and removed his body from the railing.

"Don't move," said the voice below. "Or you'll find yourself in exactly the same condition."

The second sailor looked down and saw the dark silhouette in the tender about fifteen feet below. A gun was pointed straight up at the sailor's head. The young man froze.

Denis rushed to the railing and looked below.

"Peter! You son of a bitch!" Denis yelled.

"Move back, Keyser. I've got a gun pointing at that fellow's head. If you don't do exactly as I say, I will blow his head off." Using his free hand, Sloan flicked on the tender's spotlight and pointed it at the two men by the railing, nearly blinding them.

"What the hell are you doing?" Denis exclaimed, shielding his eyes.

"I am leaving your ship. I'm afraid the voyage is over for me. By the way, don't bother trying to follow me in the other tenders. You'll find their motors are somewhat out of commission."

Denis spoke in an agitated voice. "So you're leaving now that we've found the *Sherman* site? Is that it? Who are you working for, Sloan? You goddamn son of a bitch!"

"Stay right there by the railing, Denis. Don't move. I'm going to start the tender now. If either you or that sailor moves while I'm still in sight, I'll shoot you right through the head."

Denis stood speechless. Suddenly he felt a tug at the cuff of his pants, which he had hastily put on when he heard the shot. It was Soapy Denton, crouched on the deck, an M1 rifle at his side.

Soapy whispered loud enough to be heard by Denis, although his words were inaudible to Peter Sloan over the noise of the small boat's engine. "I'll try to pick him off," Soapy said.

"Not now!" Denis protested as quietly as he could. "He could kill that sailor or me. Wait till he moves. I'll give you the signal."

Soapy nodded and lay still on the deck.

With one hand aiming the gun up toward the railing and the other on the wheel of the tender, Sloan groped at the boat's controls and turned its bow away from the hull of the *Princess*.

Sloan shouted: "Remember. Don't move or you're dead."

The tender began to chug away slowly, with Sloan steering blind, his eyes, and the gun, focusing on the two illuminated targets on the *Princess*'s deck.

Soapy, who lay out of sight, motioned to a crew member behind him to crawl up alongside. The man did, and Soapy whispered instructions to him.

Denis' pulse raced as he watched the tender pull slowly away. In a few minutes Sloan would extinguish the spotlight and his boat would be out of sight, engulfed in the darkness. Pursuit by the *Princess* was out of the question. The tender was faster and it would take at least a half hour to ready the larger ship for the chase.

Denis knew he must time his move carefully. One, possibly two lives, including his own, depended on it. He rejected the thought of simply letting Sloan escape. Sloan had already killed one sailor, and it was safe to assume that he wasn't in this alone. Somewhere, some of his fellow conspirators were hiding, waiting to be told where the *Sherman* could be found. There was no choice. Sloan must not escape.

The tender continued to slice away, its light still focused on the two men at the railing.

Denis wished he could signal to the sailor to duck on his command. But he could not take the risk of speaking to him, since his position was a good twenty feet away. The dead body of the other crew member lay at the young man's feet.

Like the ominous ticking of a clock, Denis sensed the moment approaching. He had to make his move before Sloan extinguished the spotlight and was lost in the darkness.

"Now!" Denis shouted. He lunged toward the other sailor, who hesitated a second too long. A silenced shot pierced the air, and the sailor fell, clutching his leg. The light on the tender went out and the motor increased in pitch, moving away faster.

"Lights!" Denton bellowed. He rose and aimed the M1 rifle over the side. A strong spotlight on the *Princess*'s upper deck immediately went on and scoured the area. The spotlight quickly found the tender speeding away. Denton took aim and squeezed off three noisy shots at the floodlit target. Then the spotlight on the *Princess* went out, shattered by a return shot.

Now there was silence.

"Did you get him?" Denis asked excitedly, picking himself up off the deck.

"I dunno. Maybe," Denton replied, putting the rifle down. Ahead, nothing was visible through the darkness. "We'll search the area at daybreak."

Denton moved over to where the wounded sailor was being administered to by Kualchek, the crew member who had had the medical training. "A shot in the leg, Captain," Kualchek said. "I think we can handle it." Then he pointed with his eyes to the slumped body nearby. "But Harper's dead. A clean shot through the chest."

Denton shook his head and walked toward the midship doorway. Denis followed him in.

174

"That goddamn son of a bitch," Denis said for the third time.

Colonel Cerilla chatted with Admiral Crossley in the admiral's stateroom. They sat around a small table waiting for the phone call from Washington. Both men wore khaki uniforms open at the collar. An orderly placed a small microphone and speaker on the middle of the table, the paraphernalia of a conference call.

The speaker made a noise and the sailor counted down some numbers into the microphone. When the brief test was over, the orderly turned to Admiral Crossley and said: "Ready, sir."

Crossley leaned into the microphone and boomed a greeting to his old friend the Secretary of Defense.

The Secretary responded in kind. "Deke, you old son of a gun. It's good to hear your voice. Is Colonel Cerilla there?"

"Sure is."

"Fine. Well, let's get down to business," the voice from the Pentagon said. "I'm in a bind, Colonel. I've got to produce a letter stating that all the Earhart files were declassified in 1967. Upon receipt of that letter, Amelia Earhart will reveal the details of her last flight, including the *Sherman* episode. If I don't write that letter, we're going to look pretty bad here."

Cerilla had heard the news broadcast over the destroyer's radio and was aware of the Secretary's problem. "I understand, sir," he said.

"Well, you're the Earhart expert, Colonel. What's your recommendation?"

"Mr. Secretary, could you write a letter—a simple letter authorizing Miss Earhart to reveal any details of her flight that she cared to?"

"I suppose I could do that."

"It will avoid having to confirm that 1967 declassification order, which we know was not true."

"Then what happens when she talks about the *Sherman?*"

"She won't, sir. I'm certain the woman is a fake."

There was a pause at the Washington end. "A *what!*"

Admiral Crossley looked as startled as the Secretary of Defense must have appeared halfway around the world.

"Mr. Secretary," Cerilla continued, "I've learned that one of the people on the salvage ship, Professor Peter Sloan, is in reality an agent of the People's Republic of China. In fact, he's half Chinese. His mother is a Chinese official, and his father, who died when Sloan was a boy, was an American missionary teacher. It was Sloan, I'm convinced, who gave Keyser the story of the *Sherman.*"

"What's the connection with Amelia Earhart?"

"The rest is conjecture, sir, but I'll stake my career on it. I believe that the Communist Chinese recently learned about the gold loan to Chiang Kai-shek's government. Maybe they uncovered a forgotten file. But no matter how they found out, they quickly decided to try to find the gold.

"They also knew about Earhart's mission to search for the *Sherman,* because FDR told the Chinese about it after the ship was lost. So I believe they planted this woman to try to smoke out any *Sherman* survivors who would know where the ship went down."

"I'm not sure I follow," the Secretary said.

"Remember, Mr. Secretary, that the first press release about Amelia Earhart mentioned Project Sherman. That triggered the press's interest in both Amelia Earhart and Project Sherman. Then, if what I believe is true, Peter Sloan told Keyser what Project Sherman was all about, including the loan of gold, making sure that the story hit the papers, which it did. Today we know that Sloan is a Chinese agent and just happens to be on the ship that's searching for the *Sherman.* It's too pat, sir. I'm sure the Chinese set the whole thing up to find the gold."

The Secretary "hmmmed" on the phone. "I'm beginning to get the picture, Colonel. I suppose, then, that Mr. Sloan's role is to pinpoint the ship for his Chinese friends. Then what happens?"

"I can only guess at that, sir. But I don't think I'd like to be a passenger on the salvage ship right now."

"All right, Colonel. I'll write a letter authorizing Mrs. Stenemond to say anything she pleases. In fact, I'll insist that her doctor come here and get it himself. That'll give some of your boys a chance to talk to him at some length. Maybe the doctor can shed some more light on all this."

"I think that's a fine idea," Cerilla said.

"What's the salvage ship's position, Deke?" asked the voice on the speaker.

"About forty miles ahead of us, sir," Admiral Crossley replied. "Just off Pingelap atoll. That may be the salvage spot, because they've been dead in the water for a while."

"Well, forget about hanging back, Deke. You'd better get over to the salvage site and show the flag. Let's protect our interests."

"Yes, sir."

"Good luck, gentlemen" were the final words from Washington.

chapter
21

"I guess we missed all the excitement last night," Jason said when he ran into Denis on his way to the *Princess's* wheelhouse.

"Yeah. We've got one less passenger this morning." Then Denis added in a more sober tone, "And one dead sailor."

Jason shook his head. "I still can't believe it. Where did Sloan go?"

"We don't know for sure. We searched the area at dawn but found no trace of him or the tender he stole. But it's still possible that Soapy hit him and the tender drifted away."

"Well, I'd better get up to the wheelhouse," Jason said. "It's my turn to be useful. Keep an eye on Peggy, would you, Denis? I'm afraid she had a bad night."

"Sure," Denis replied, figuring out why they had not been roused by the evening's commotion. It had been another night at the bottle for Peggy Allenby and friend.

Soapy Denton and two sailors were waiting for Jason when he climbed the ladder to the ship's wheelhouse. As usual, Soapy had a large ugly cigar in his mouth.

"All right, Caldwell," Soapy said unceremoniously. "I'm

going to position the ship at the site you remember best, okay?" From the wheelhouse's vantage point, Pingelap atoll and the hilly shape of the dinosaur dominated the horizon.

Jason gazed out the window, taking in the sight of the balmy island surrounded by deep blue water. "We were in closer than this," he said.

"Check. We'll cruise back and forth, parallel to the beach, moving closer ashore, while you remember where you were when the explosion hit. You got that?"

Jason nodded.

"When you think we've hit the spot, you sound off."

On Denton's command, the ship turned and cut slowly through the water, following a course along Pingelap's sandy beach.

Jason continued to stare at the island, saying nothing.

After four passes back and forth, at increasingly closer distances to the beach, Jason had still not spoken and Denton's patience was ebbing. "Well, Caldwell, did your fucking ship sail right onto the shore?"

Jason ignored him.

On the sixth pass, about halfway along the beach at a distance of seven-eights of a mile, Jason turned around and simply said: "Stop."

Soapy gave the order, and the ship gradually slowed to a halt.

"I think this is it," Jason announced.

"Depth!" Soapy barked.

A sailor checked one of the gauges on the wide panel by the wheel.

"Three hundred feet, sir."

"Deploy the side-scanner magnometer."

"Aye, aye, sir."

On deck, two sailors lifted a small rocketlike object about three feet long and heaved it overboard. A connecting coil uncurled rapidly as the object sank to the bottom.

Soapy motioned to Jason, who had watched the operation with considerable interest. "That's the magnometer," Soapy said. "We'll start here and crisscross the area. If the 'fish' detects any large accumulation of metal, it'll register on the graph over there."

Behind them stood a machine with a nervous automatic pencil that made marks on graph paper as the paper slowly wound by. Jason acknowledged the technical achievement, as he did all such electronic gadgets, with a shrug.

"No reading, sir," a bearded technician announced.

"Okay, let's get moving."

The *Princess*'s engines roared to a start and the slow process of searching for the *Sherman* began. With the magnometer trailing behind at the end of its tether, the *Princess* sailed back and forth, following the contours of the island at varying distances. As they moved, the black pencil vacillated on the graph paper, tracing a wiggling line that meant there was no metal below.

The meandering seemed endless. They turned for the sixth time, retracing another ocean path, while the warm sun rose in the sky and beat down on them.

Finally, after two hours of searching, a light flashed on the magnometer's console. The graph pencil, which had moved only slightly until now, gyrated frantically in wide arcs from one end of the graph paper to the other.

The bearded technician who was monitoring the machine at the rear of the wheelhouse flashed a thumbs-up signal to Soapy Denton, whose hands were at the *Princess*'s wheel.

"All stop!" Denton ordered.

He surveyed their position. The ship was now located opposite the beach at about the same position Jason had originally identified, only now they were a half mile farther out.

Denton sounded off: "Depth!"

"Three hundred and fifty feet, sir."

"What have we got?"

The technician grinned. "We've got one hell of a lot of metal, Captain. Could easily be a ship."

"Prepare the saucer for a dive," Denton ordered into a

microphone. His voice echoed around the ship's decks. "I'll go down with Thorpe."

On deck, three sailors removed a tarpaulin from the three-ton diving saucer. The contraption was aptly named, resembling, as it did, the most common conception of a science-fiction flying saucer. This one held two humans and had a bubble top. It was self-propelled and equipped with remote-television cameras as well as underwater feelers and sensing devices. Once submerged, the saucer could remain below up to two hours at a depth of up to 450 feet.

Jason lumbered up to the wheelhouse as soon as he noticed the sailors readying the diving saucer for action.

"Can I go along on the dive?" Jason asked.

"This ain't no sightseeing cruise, Caldwell. First, it's dangerous. Second, we've got work to do down there. You can watch us on TV in the Control Center."

The divers' Control Center was the only place on the ship where even Soapy Denton obediently followed instructions. Its master was Dr. Marshall Creuset, an expert on all phases of deep-sea diving. Creuset, half French and half American, had served several years with Jacques Cousteau until he decided he would rather be based in California than on the drizzly coast of France. Denton wasted no time signing him on, despite the fact that Creuset's price was high. Divers' lives depended on Creuset's decisions, so in that job Soapy figured he could afford nothing but the best, at any price. Creuset was forty-two, bald and skinny, a spindle of a man. But when he spoke, he did so with commanding authority.

"I'll tell Dr. Creuset you're going to monitor the dive with him," Soapy said, in a soft voice for a change.

Jason joined Dr. Creuset in the cramped Control Center while Soapy and his men made final preparations for the dive. Clad in their normal clothes, since the saucer was fully pressurized, Denton and Thorpe climbed into the small submarine and closed the bubble top, sealing it into place. On Denton's signal, the saucer, attached securely to a winch, was slowly lowered into the water. There, the chains were released, the saucer's internal engine started, and the eerie contraption slowly sank into the ocean.

In the Control Center Dr. Creuset switched on three television sets and spoke softly into a microphone. Two of the video screens displayed an underwater view of the area in front of the saucer. The third screen provided an image of the saucer's two occupants.

"One hundred feet." Denton's voice sounded over a small loudspeaker.

"Change the air mixture to formula three-five-zero," Creuset ordered.

"Roger," Denton acknowledged.

Through the plastic top of the bubble, Denton and Thorpe gazed silently at the underwater panorama. The strong lights of the saucer illuminated a rich scene of hundreds of fish of all sizes, some large and awesome, others vividly colorful, a maritime surrealistic painting.

"Three hundred feet," Denton announced.

"Look below," Thorpe said, pointing.

Slowly, through the dark depths of the water, the saucer's lights caught the outline of a ship lying on her side at the bottom.

"Can you see it up there?" Denton asked.

Dr. Creuset and Jason stared at the television screens and saw the hazy but identifiable form of a ship.

"We see it, Soapy," Dr. Creuset said.

"Looks like it could be a Navy ship to me," Soapy advised. "I'm going to steer the saucer to the bow."

"Roger."

The camera stayed fixed on the ship as Denton maneuvered the saucer to the wreck's bow. The iron plates of the vessel's hull were deeply encrusted with oysters, barnacles, and other marine growth. The ship had obviously been submerged for a very long time.

"I'm going to use one of the sensors and try to scrape some of the growth off the bow," Denton said. "I want to find the name, if possible."

"Go ahead. You've got some time."

The scraping started in earnest but revealed nothing.

"Whew. There's a lot of junk encrusted on that wreck," Thorpe commented.

After an hour of arduous scraping by the mechanical arm protruding from the saucer, Soapy Denton cheerfully announced: "We've hit a letter."

In the Control Center, Dr. Creuset and Jason Caldwell stared at the video screens. "It looks like an E," Jason said.

"E is correct," Thorpe acknowledged from below.

Dr. Creuset spoke up. "Time's almost up, gentlemen."

"One more letter, Marshall. Just to be sure."

"Okay. Hurry."

The scratching and scraping continued. The next letter revealed a straight line. The rest of the scraping unveiled the full letter R.

"We've got it!" Soapy yelled, and his voice, along with Thorpe's, mixed into an unintelligible but enthusiastic noise over the small speaker in the Control Center.

Dr. Creuset's voice, however, held no emotion: "You can celebrate later. Get back up. Your time's run out."

It was a joyous group gathered around the table in the mess. Soapy sat at the head with a smiling Thorpe at his right. Dr. Creuset was there. Denis Keyser took notes for the story he would file. Peggy Allenby and Jason Caldwell held hands and beamed.

"You did it, Jason," Soapy said with a grin. "And I'm proud of you."

Jason smiled and squeezed Peggy's hand.

"Now comes the hard part," Soapy continued. "The ship's at three hundred and fifty feet. That's tricky business for a diver."

"Can it be done?" Denis asked.

Dr. Creuset replied. "It can, but it will require special procedures. And it is dangerous. I presume we'll have to cut through some part of the ship to get at the cargo."

All eyes looked to Jason, who coughed nervously before speaking. "The gold should be in the forward hold, on the port side. That's hold number two. We all knew that our secret cargo was there and it was off-limits. I'll draw a sketch for you, Soapy."

"How much cutting will we have to do?" Soapy asked.

"If you cut from the top, probably just one steel plate about an inch thick, I'd guess." Jason traced the outline of a ship on a piece of paper, marked an X in one spot, and slid the paper across the table to Soapy.

Dr. Creuset scratched his head. "The divers will use triple tanks with a helium-nitrogen-oxygen mixture to prevent narcosis. We'll also have to use the SDC."

Denis stopped writing on his pad and looked up. "What's that?"

Soapy rose. "C'mon outside. You'll see. Let's get this show on the road."

When they arrived on deck, Denis saw a tubular-shaped container, about twelve feet tall, hanging from a winch. A sailor was in the process of attaching a heavy weight to the bottom of the contraption. Dr. Creuset joined Denton and Keyser as they watched the activity.

"That's the SDC," Denton said. "It stands for Submersible Decompression Chamber. We'll drop it halfway down to the wreck and hold it there. On the way up, the divers will go into the SDC for decompression while we gradually change the air mixture back to normal."

"How long will that take?" Denis asked. A sea breeze whipped around the deck and felt good against the hot rays of the sun.

"About three hours," Dr. Creuset said. "But we'll haul the SDC back up on deck and then change the air mixture."

"Ready, Captain," a sailor yelled from beneath the SDC. Soapy cupped his hands at his mouth: "Let 'er go!"

With a grinding noise the winch lifted the empty SDC and rotated on its axis until the device and its trailing weight were hanging over the side of the ship. Then the capsule was slowly lowered into the ocean, where it would await the divers on their way back up from the bottom.

"How much working time, Marshall?" Denton asked.

"No more than fifteen minutes, I'm afraid."

Denis looked puzzled. "You mean for every fifteen minutes' work these divers will take three hours to come up?"

"Now you know why we like to get paid by the hour," Denton quipped. "I've got to get suited up." He left the other two men and headed inside.

Dr. Creuset and Denis were still on deck when Soapy returned in his wet suit and fins. Two other divers, Roger Dolan and Larry Reich, followed him at close range. Each man wore three air tanks on his back.

"Where are the underwater torches?" Soapy asked.

"Over here, Captain." Dolan opened a wooden chest by the railing. He pulled out two acetylene torches, each with its own small fuel tank. "They were checked out in the machine shop this morning."

"I'll take one of the torches," Soapy said. "Roger, you take the other."

A second winch ground into gear, this one attached to the saucer submarine. Thorpe ambled over to the sub, whose plastic canopy was open.

Soapy yelled over to him. "Take the sub below. When you're in place, we'll swim down."

Thorpe acknowledged the instructions and climbed into the saucer. The winch rotated and positioned the small vessel over the side before slowly lowering it to the water. Dr. Creuset left the group to assume his duties in the Control Center, where he would monitor the functioning of the saucer sub and the Submersible Decompression Chamber.

The saucer had been submerged for several minutes when word came from Dr. Creuset that Thorpe was in position and ready. On Soapy's signal, he and the two other divers jumped into the water and slowly began their descent, following the line holding the SDC in place. As they descended into the quiet of the deep, the daylight from above grew dim, until it gradually disappeared, leaving them in darkness. Now the powerful light beams from the saucer sub were visible below, and the three divers quietly swam toward it.

185

Below the sub lay the imposing, barnacle-encrusted carcass of the *Sherman*. It was more impressive to Soapy from this vantage point, where he could walk on the ship, enter her interior, and touch her hull under the sea growth that had accumulated over a period of forty years. This was real diving, Soapy thought, as he exhaled a breath of the helium-hydrogen-oxygen mixture, sending a stream of bubbles floating up around his mask. Compared to this experience, seeing the wreck from the saucer was nothing more than a spectator sport, and by nature Soapy was more of a participant than a spectator.

Using hand signals, Soapy led Dolan and Reich to the position Jason had marked for him. The *Sherman* lay on her side, and as they swam by, Soapy observed the gaping hole in the ship's middle. They had been hit by a torpedo, all right.

In the Control Center, Dr. Creuset monitored the activities carefully and spoke to Thorpe in the sub. So far, everything was proceeding smoothly.

Suddenly two white sharks appeared in view, their ominous fins pointing straight at the divers. Soapy and the other men froze, hoping not to attract their attention. The sharks swam within ten feet of Soapy, and he wondered if they had caught the scent, or were hungry, or afraid. He held his breath. The sharks turned away and decided to roam elsewhere.

When the predators were safely out of range, the three divers headed for their target: hold number two. Soapy got there first and banged the back of his diving knife on the metal plate. It clanged against the blow. The saucer maneuvered in closer, beaming its two streams of light toward the divers.

Denton pointed to the spot where they would cut the metal. He glanced at his diver's watch. They had eight minutes left.

Roger Dolan fired his torch and went to work. Soapy did the same, and attacked another area of the steel plate. Later he could join up with Dolan's incision. Around them the quiet ghost of a ship lay dead, resting in her underwater grave of forty years.

Dolan cut through first, and a flood of water suddenly whooshed into the hole, toppling him temporarily. As the hold filled with water, Denton and Dolan cut a man-size hole with their torches, working toward each other to complete the circle. When their incisions met, they lifted the round piece of metal and tossed it aside while the third diver aimed his flashlight down the hole. There, below them, was a gleaming, beautiful stack of shiny gold bars.

"Time's up!" Dr. Creuset shouted in the microphone. "What the hell are they doing?"

Thorpe responded by blinking the sub's lights, a warning to Denton and his men that they must start back up to the SDC.

Denton waved and extended a forefinger to the sub and its television cameras.

"He seems to want one more minute," Thorpe said.

"No!" Dr. Creuset shouted.

But Soapy had disappeared down the hole into hold number two. Dolan and Reich began their ascent to the SDC while Thorpe nervously awaited Soapy's reappearance.

What first emerged from the hole, by the light of the saucer sub's beams and on the TV screens in the Control Center, was not Soapy Denton's face, but an extended hand in which a gold bar shimmered and gleamed.

"That's it!" Jason cried, as he monitored the proceedings on the screen, looking over Dr. Creuset's shoulder.

"Get up, Soapy, goddammit," Creuset hissed through clenched teeth.

Slowly Denton ascended to the SDC and entered the water lock. The water was then forced out of the compartment and Soapy joined his two colleagues in the dry comfort of the SDC's cylindrical chamber.

Dr. Creuset breathed a sigh of relief. He made some quick calculations, adjusted the air and pressure inside the SDC, then ordered the capsule lifted onto the ship. There the men would remain for three hours while the decompression process ran its course.

When the capsule was tightly fastened to the deck, Dr. Creuset initiated voice contact with the divers.

"Congratulations, Soapy," he said calmly.

"Marshall, I am holding the most beautiful piece of metal you've ever seen. And there's hundreds of them down there!"

"We'll get them all."

"You there, Caldwell? We're rich, you old bastard," Denton chortled. "You hear me? I said *rich!*"

Jason responded with glee. "I heard you, Soapy."

When Denton popped out of the SDC after the mandatory three-hour confinement, he still had a handsome grin on his face and a gold bar in his hand. He passed the gold bar around, to the delight of dozens of ogling eyes among the crew on deck.

"Okay, back to work!" Soapy ordered. "We're going down again."

Dr. Creuset shook his head. He didn't like the idea of back-to-back dives at that depth, but Soapy and his men had been fully decompressed, so there was no compelling medical reason, besides fatigue, to prevent them from diving again.

Soapy moved around the deck barking orders. "Marshall, alert Thorpe that we're coming down again, okay? Johnson, get a large metal basket hooked up to a line. I want it lowered to the wreck to hoist the gold bars up. Okay, everybody, let's move!"

On cue, the crew hastily went about assigned duties, preparing the SDC for submersion, refilling the air tanks, checking lines and chains, refitting the diving suits. Dr. Creuset repaired to the Control Center and radioed Thorpe, who was still below, that he was to remain in the saucer sub to monitor another dive.

On deck, Soapy Denton, Roger Dolan, and Larry Reich checked one another's gear.

"I figure it'll take a dozen or so more dives to get it all up, fifteen minutes at a time," Soapy said. "We'd better have another diving team standing by when we come out of the SDC."

The other two men agreed, and Dolan relayed the instructions to a colleague, who would get the message to Creuset.

Now the three divers were ready. They bit into their mouthpieces and backflipped into the water. As they descended, the water turned darker, until they had passed the last glimmer of daylight and were engulfed in darkness. Below, the lights from the saucer sub were a welcome sight.

Soapy and his two men swam past the saucer sub, following the rays of its powerful lights, two beacons pointing straight to the hole they had opened in the hulk of the *Sherman*. The old ship, lying on its side, seemed as drab and lifeless as before.

Denton yearned to cast his eyes on the rich color of gold down below. As they approached the wreck, he looked around at the myriad variety of fish swimming by. He recalled only too well the close encounter with the sharks on the last dive. He didn't think his heart could take any more surprises like that.

The three divers arrived at the opening in the hold and pointed their flashlights down, assuring themselves that the gold was still there. It was, and the bars gleamed at them, an undulating, out-of-focus vision rippling through the floodlit water. Dolan searched the area for the suspended metal basket. He found it only a few feet away. Reich, who was the thinnest diver, squeezed into the hold and swam to the cache of gold bars. While Denton and Dolan watched, Reich picked up two bars and struggled to swim back up, but the weight of the gold made his ascent slow and painful. He kicked hard, moving his fins back and forth, and ever so slowly rose to the opening above. Denton reached down the hole and grabbed Reich's arm as he approached. Soapy relieved the diver of the gold bars and handed them to Dolan, who put them in the metal basket suspended near him. Then Reich swam back down to the bottom of the hold.

As soon as he reached the stack of gold bars, Soapy held up his forefinger, a signal that Reich understood immediately: bring up only one bar at a time.

In the saucer sub, Thorpe monitored the activity meticulously, remaining in constant voice contact with Creuset in the *Princess*'s Control Center. The lights from the sub illuminated the area where Denton and Dolan were visibly working.

Suddenly Thorpe saw something in the distance. He gazed through the bubble's plexiglass top and soon saw two powerful lights approaching him. He spoke into the microphone in an agitated voice.

"Marshall, there's something down here. I see lights."

"Maybe it's a reflection."

"No. It must be another sub. But from where, for God's sake?"

"Stay calm," Creuset exhorted. "I'll tell you exactly what to do. First, I want you to flash the danger signal to the divers."

Thorpe did so. Three long blinks followed by two short ones. This time, Denton wasted no time heeding the signal, a warning of imminent danger. He pointed to the basket, which now had five bars in it, and Thorpe gave the order to hoist it up. Then Soapy, Dolan, and Reich began their ascent to the SDC, which was suspended underwater about two hundred feet above. The second pair of lights was now visible to all of them.

"I see it now," Thorpe exclaimed. "It's another two-man saucer. Hold it! There's some divers swimming alongside. Three! No, four divers! They've got spear guns!"

"Where's Denton?" Creuset demanded.

"They're working their way up to the SDC."

The second submarine, its lights illuminating the way, moved toward the wreck of the *Sherman*, flanked by four armed divers. As the sub approached the site, its lights caught the basket of gold rising at the end of its wire. The four divers broke away from the submarine and swam toward the basket.

From their position a few feet higher, Denton tapped Dolan's shoulder and pointed down. Below them, the other divers were reaching for the basket of gold. Soapy tugged at the line holding the basket in a futile attempt to move it away from the predators.

"Get up to the SDC!" Thorpe shouted from the sub, although, of course, the divers could not hear him. He aimed his beams at the action ahead, bathing the four unknown divers in light.

The basket jerked away just as one of the armed divers reached for it. The man looked about while a colleague pointed a flashlight. In seconds, their beam caught Soapy, who was frantically waving them off, like a traffic cop at a busy intersection. Without hesitation the armed diver raised his spear gun and fired. A long, pointed arrow cut through the water, dangling a string behind it.

"Marshall, they've fired at Soapy. I've got to do something." But what? Thorpe wondered. He watched the spear miss and breathed a sigh of relief as he observed his friends swimming away, heading for the SDC. Two of the enemy divers gave pursuit, aiming their spear guns as they swam.

"They're chasing our men. I'm going after them," Thorpe announced into his microphone. The sub's engine revved up, Thorpe engaged the forward gear, and the small craft took off. The other sub remained with the two men by the gold, its pilots not caring what Thorpe might do, since none of the small submersible craft of that type carried any weapons.

It was a matter of seconds. Above, the group consisting of Denton, Reich, and Dolan was swimming toward the SDC and relative safety. Behind them, two men with spear guns pursued at a fast clip while Thorpe pushed the sub in closer, its lights glued to the two predators.

When he was but a few feet away from one of the armed divers, Thorpe pulled the lever to deploy a metal clamp attached to the bottom of his craft. The clamp swung out and locked into position, its jaws open wide. Normally the clamps were used to move underwater finds and to assist in breaking apart large pieces of wreckage. The clamp's jagged teeth assured an ironclad bite. Today it would have to serve a different purpose.

As Thorpe approached, the armed divers turned to face the small sub and its powerful lights. Until now they had ignored the small vessel, knowing, as did their colleagues, that the sub would not be armed and hence posed no real danger to them. They changed their minds about that when they saw the metal clamp whose threatening razor-sharp teeth suddenly took on new meaning.

Thorpe picked out one of the armed divers and maneuvered toward him, manipulating the sub's controls with great finesse. He yelled at his enemy, psyching himself up, while Creuset listened helplessly in the *Princess's* Control Center.

The diver banged the butt of his spear gun against the plexiglass, hoping to shatter it, but to no avail.

"Now!" Thorpe shouted. He swerved the clamp around and caught the diver's leg. He thrust forward the lever that closed the clamp. The steel jaws instantly locked around the man's thigh, sending spurts of black blood oozing through the water. The diver dropped his spear gun and flailed frantically like a decapitated hen. In less than a minute he was still.

"I'm going after the others!" Thorpe shouted, his mind intoxicated by the initial victory.

"No!" Creuset ordered. "One of them may go for your propellers!"

The logic of Creuset's comment hit Thorpe like a cold splash of water. Creuset was right, of course. If one of the enemy divers tampered with the saucer sub's screws,

Thorpe would no longer be able to navigate. He would be at their mercy; a chilling thought.

"All right," Thorpe announced. "I'm coming up." He directed the sub to the surface and began his ascent. A few seconds later Creuset confirmed over the intercom that Denton, Reich, and Dolan were secure in the SDC, which was in the process of being raised to the *Princess's* deck.

For the first time in many tension-filled minutes Thorpe took his hands off the sub's controls. He could not stop his fingers from shaking.

chapter
22

Colonel Cerilla sipped his coffee slowly. The brew was hot and strong, a welcome tonic at sea. He and Admiral Crossley stood on the bridge surveying the wide expanse of ocean that lay before them.

"We should be at Pingelap in under an hour, at this rate," Crossley commented. "That salvage ship hasn't budged all day. They may have found it."

Cerilla nodded. He had long ago accepted the possibility that the *Sherman* would be discovered. And then what? he wondered. The government would make a legal case to get the gold back, and it would be a strong case. But was there a jury anywhere in the world that would sympathize with the Pentagon's side of this story? Or any story, for that matter. Cerilla took another sip of the black coffee and tried to think more positive thoughts.

The watch officer from the Combat Information Center appeared, the latest satellite-radar report in his hand. "There's something going on out there, sir," he said ominously.

Admiral Crossley put his coffee mug down and motioned to a nearby table covered with charts. "Let's have a look."

Cerilla joined the senior officer at the chart table while the lieutenant unfurled the computer-prepared satellite readout.

"Right there, sir," the lieutenant said, pointing with a pencil at one of the marks on the paper. "Here's the *Princess* just behind Pingelap. Now, over here, another ship has appeared. It seems to be stopped on the other side of the atoll."

"Hmmm. Is it one of ours?"

"No, sir. We'd have had a transponder ID signal if it were. It's foreign."

"Do you have any ideas, Colonel?" Crossley asked, turning to Cerilla.

"Yes, sir. I'd guess it was Chinese. It fits in with the information about Sloan. Sounds like they're playing cat and mouse out there."

"Well, the other ship will have to contact the *Princess* sooner or later. What then?"

"They may simply ask Denton and his party to leave."

"And if they don't?"

Colonel Cerilla just shrugged, but the meaning behind his gesture was apparent. Crossley turned to the duty officer on the bridge.

"Richards, I want every ounce of speed you can get out of this ship, and I want it now!"

** AUGUST 4 ** AP—High officials at the Pentagon have authorized Mrs. Emily Stenemond, who claims to be Amelia Earhart, to reveal any information about Earhart's last flight, the Chicago *Tribune* reported today. Mrs. Stenemond, who had earlier refused to discuss Earhart's last flight, agreed to do so if authorized by the Department of Defense. A letter from the Secretary of Defense releasing Amelia Earhart from any oath of secrecy was delivered yesterday to Richard J. Townsend, a Chicago *Tribune* reporter, and Dr. James C. Wilton, Mrs. Stenemond's physician. Wilton stated that Mrs. Stenemond would hold a press conference within a week.

-o-

"I don't believe it!" Dr. Wilton said, while a look of fear spread over his face. He slumped into the chair beside the desk of Dr. Raymond Manchester, the Medical Institute's executive director.

"I'm afraid it's so." Manchester sighed. He was a man of about sixty who had faced many problems and crises in his long tenure at the Institute, but never one like this.

"Have you searched everywhere?" Wilton pleaded.

"Everywhere. She's gone. Vanished."

"I was away for only one day!" Wilton blurted, his face now a bright pink. "To get this damned letter." He waved the letter under Manchester's nose. "This Institute couldn't keep its eyes on her for one day?"

"Now, see here, Doctor," Manchester said, stiffening. "This is a medical institution, not a prison. Mrs. Stenemond was free to leave at any time, and apparently she did just that."

"But without my authorization you let... Oh, God, what's the use," Wilton moaned, his flat Australian accent thickening with every sentence. "Who saw her last?"

"One of the nurses. I understand Mrs. Stenemond left her room with an unidentified middle-aged woman. She carried only a large bag and she smiled at the nurse on her way down the corridor."

"She didn't say where she was going?"

"No. She merely departed, and she has not returned."

"Colonel Cerilla? There's a TWX here from Washington, sir." The radioman handed a yellow envelope to the Army officer. "It's unclassified, Colonel. Apparently Amelia Earhart has vanished."

A wry smile formed on Colonel Cerilla's lips. While he was reading the message from Captain Turner, Admiral Crossley burst into the stateroom. The lieutenant snapped to attention.

"I heard the news," Crossley said.

"I'm not really surprised, Admiral." Cerilla's voice resonated in a tone of self-confidence. "The Chinese know where the *Sherman* is now. Mrs. Stenemond's job is done.

She smoked out a *Sherman* survivor who led them to the wreck."

"I know we've had this discussion before, Colonel, but I still don't see why they had to go to all that trouble."

"Because, sir," Cerilla added eagerly, "bringing Amelia Earhart back was the only practical way for the Chinese to reach a *Sherman* survivor. We know that Roosevelt told the Chinese about Earhart's mission to find the ship. He probably also told them that Earhart saw some survivors, although she was never able to radio the location. So if the Chinese today were to have any chance to get the gold, they would have to find a *Sherman* survivor who might remember where the ship went down."

Admiral Crossley shook his head. "Surely there must have been an easier way to find one of those men!"

"Not really. Had the Chinese made any overt attempt to track down a *Sherman* crew member, we'd have been on their tail right away. No, the Chinese had to get one of the survivors to come forward on *his* own and lead them to the gold. Bringing Earhart back started a preplanned chain of events that accomplished just that."

The Admiral seemed only partly convinced. "Well, it must have been one hell of a job to train an old woman to impersonate Amelia Earhart."

"Yes, sir. A Herculean task. But I'm convinced that the Chinese did it."

The destroyer heaved slightly, moving at high speed through the choppy water.

"If your theory's correct, Colonel, we ought to be meeting some Chinese, eyeball to eyeball, in a little while. According to the last satellite report, the unidentified ship is circling around the atoll and is just about to make visual contact with the *Princess*."

chapter
23

Two and a half hours after the SDC had been hauled onto deck, the divers waited restlessly for their second confinement to end. A young sailor entered the Control Center and asked Dr. Creuset if he could speak to the captain.

"Sure. Talk into the microphone here."

"Captain?" the young man began. "This is Hanna, sir. There's something I thought you oughta know. Radar's picked up a ship. It must have been on the other side of the atoll, but now it looks like it's swinging around and heading toward us."

"Goddammit!" Denton cursed. He pounded on the thick plexiglass that separated him from the outside world. "That's where those divers came from. Marshall! Get me out of this thing!"

A few feet away, Dr. Creuset sat calmly, monitoring the portable instruments connected to the SDC. He glanced at his watch. "Another ten minutes, Soapy. Be patient."

"Has anybody sighted that ship yet?" Denton hollered into the intercom.

A sailor peered through massive binoculars and braced

himself against the railing. "I see it, Captain! She's steaming straight toward us."

Creuset relayed the message to the SDC, where Soapy reacted as impatiently as before. "I want out, Marshall!"

"Soapy, if you don't shut up, I'm going to turn the intercom off."

"I can make it out now," the lookout announced, his eyes glued to the binoculars. "It looks like a small destroyer —probably a frigate."

"The U.S. Navy?" Creuset asked.

"No, sir. Doesn't look American. I should be able to spot the flag when she gets a little closer."

The seconds ticked away interminably, until finally, on Dr. Creuset's command, the SDC was opened and Soapy Denton jumped out first. He marched straight over to the railing where the sailor was following the alien ship, now clearly visible to the naked eye.

"Let me have the glasses," Soapy ordered, and took them away from the young man. Now a flock of crew members and divers had gathered on deck, some equipped with their own binoculars. Denis Keyser, Jason, and Peggy were among them. They stared silently at the growing gray form steaming toward them, a black stream of smoke trailing behind.

"I can just make out the flag," one observer declared. "It's all red with some markings in the corner."

Denton peered into the glasses at the unfriendly vessel. "That's the flag of the People's Republic of China."

Denis, who had observed the proceedings silently until now, took Jason and Peggy aside. "This could get rough," he announced in a low voice. "If there's a fight, you two better be prepared to evacuate. I don't know about you, but I've got no intention of becoming a martyr for a stack of gold bars."

Peggy shook her head violently. "It's our gold," she said through clenched teeth. "They can't take it away from us. They can't!"

The dark gray frigate, her twin cannon ominously uncovered, came to a stop in the water about three hundred yards away from the *Princess*. Over at the railing, one of the crew members who was equipped with binoculars motioned to Denis to come over. "Here's a sight you won't believe," he said.

Denis looked through the glasses and adjusted the focus while the sailor directed his vision along the destroyer's bridge to the spot he wanted Denis to look at.

"Have you got the bridge?"

"Yeah," Denis said. "Bunch of people in uniform. Chinese, it looks like."

"Look at the third fellow from the left. Not in uniform. The one with the arm in a sling."

Denis followed the instruction and gazed. "Well, I'll be damned," he said, as he made out the familiar shape of Peter Sloan. "So that's who the bastard was working for. The Chinese!" Denis noticed the sling and was cheered by it. At least one of Soapy's shots had found its mark.

"They're flashing us on the signal light!"

"Doores, take down the message," Denton ordered. Doores, a communications specialist, pulled a pencil and a small wire-bound notebook from his pants pocket and began transcribing the Morse-code letters transmitted by the flashing of the frigate's signal light.

While the group hovered impatiently nearby, Doores took the message down, letter by letter, until the blinking finally stopped. Then he read aloud.

"They say: 'You are on the site of property owned by the People's Republic of China. You are responsible for the death of one of our crew. You must leave at once or suffer grave consequences.'"

Denis grabbed Soapy Denton's arm. "For Christ's sake, Soapy, let's get out of here!"

Denton jerked his arm away angrily. His face boiled with rage. "Flash this message back," he demanded in a voice of controlled anger. "'We are situated in international waters. We have a right to be here, and we are not moving.'"

"Denton!" Denis shouted. "You are out of your fucking mind! You can't take on a warship, you dumb bastard!"

"Get out of my way!" Denton yelled with contempt. As he spoke, his message began to flicker on the portable flasher, beaming its way to the Chinese frigate.

"Well, I'm taking one of the tenders and getting off this ship," Denis announced. He silently thanked the Almighty for the fact that the tenders had been repaired following Sloan's attempt to put them out of commission. "Jason and Peggy—you're coming with me. Don't stay here with this madman."

"I'm afraid Denis is right," Jason said, putting his arm around Peggy. "Let's get our things."

"You go ahead," Peggy said. "I'll meet you at the tender in three minutes."

Denis grabbed his passport, his camera, and all of his notes and shoved them into a duffel bag. He stripped a blanket off the bunk, figuring it might come in handy if he were marooned for an extended period. On the way out, he stopped by the galley and took a dozen cans of food and some vegetables and fruits from the refrigerator; then, as an afterthought, he picked up a metal can opener. In any event, Denis reasoned that if worse came to worst, they could always head toward Pingelap and survive there for as long as it took to get rescued. For the first time, Denis regretted all of the snide remarks he had made in his youth about boy scouts. At this stage of his life, Denis Keyser knew virtually nothing about survival in the wilderness.

Jason was already waiting by the tender when Denis hurried up, his duffel bag trailing behind him.

"Where's Peggy?" Denis asked.

"I don't know," Jason said, worried.

"I'll go look for her."

Denis found her alongside Soapy Denton while they monitored the slow transmission of their Morse-code message to the frigate. "C'mon, Peggy," Denis said. "We're leaving now."

"I'm not going," she announced.

Denis reached for her arm, but Peggy pulled away, moving closer to Denton. "Go ahead, Denis. Leave, and take Jason with you. You can't possibly understand."

"What's there to understand? You can get killed staying here!"

Peggy began to sob. "Go away," she pleaded. "Please. I have nothing to go back to. I have no job! I have no money! The gold was going to finance my new life. I can't give it up!"

Suddenly a bright light flashed from the bow of the frigate. Seconds later the crew and passengers of the *Princess* heard the boom of the ship's cannon and the explosion of the shell about fifty yards in front of them, a gushy spout of water blowing straight up out of the ocean.

Denton yelled an order: "Get out the rifles!"

"Peggy! Now do you understand?" Denis shouted. "This is your last chance. Let's go!"

"*No! No! No!*" she cried.

Another flash of light sparked the horizon, followed by the slower arrival of the sound of the shot, and another spray of water burst before them. Denis raced around the deck to the tender, where Jason struggled to loosen the boat from the winch.

"Where's Peggy?" Jason asked.

Denis didn't reply. He attacked the winch and finally got the small boat lowered to the water. "Jump in, Jason."

"But what about Peggy?"

The sound of another shot reverberated around them, and this time the shell hit fifty yards behind the *Princess*.

"They're bracketing us! We've only got a few minutes left, Jason!"

"I can't leave without Peggy!" Jason pleaded.

In desperation Denis pushed Jason toward the railing and made him climb over to the other side. Then Denis shoved him into the water, a drop of about fifteen feet. Jason paddled awkwardly but made enough movement to stay afloat, while Denis lowered himself to the tender.

Just before Denis started the small boat's engine, he heard Soapy's deep voice bellowing a command to zigzag out of the frigate's line of fire.

Jason climbed into the boat, shivering and out of breath. He lay panting on the wooden seat, an arm hanging over the side. Denis detached the last support hook from the winch, fired the engine, and swerved the small craft away from the *Princess* at high speed. As he did, another shot exploded behind the *Princess*.

"You'll never get away in time, Soapy," Denis yelled into the wind and the spray that pelleted his face. "You dumb, obstinate bastard!"

As Denis knew from a story he once wrote about field artillery, while still in journalism school, it was common practice to "bracket" your target, one shot at a time, when using heavy artillery. You fired one shot long, then another shot short, closing the gap each time. Then, when you were pretty sure you had the right range and bearing, you fired "for effect," unleashing all the ammunition you needed to destroy the objective. It was a primitive system of artillery, but the Chinese were still using it.

As they skipped along the water at high speed, Denis rubbed his eyes, trying to shield them from the spray. The vision he saw ahead was not reassuring to him. "Jesus," he moaned. "Another ship."

The men in khaki uniforms assumed identical poses, feet apart to maintain balance, hands held up to steady the binoculars in place. From the bridge of the destroyer *Admiral Crossley*, Colonel Cerilla, and two watch officers assessed the sights unfolding before them.

"That frigate is firing at the salvage ship!" Crossley yelled. "Get me an identification."

An officer and two sailors scurried about, consulting large looseleaf books with warship nomenclature.

"It's a Russian frigate, sir," the officer announced. "Riga class."

"This one's flying a Chinese flag, though," Crossley said, still gazing through the binoculars. "What's her armament?"

"Three 3.9-inch single guns and four thirty-seven-millimeter cannon. She's using the cannon right now."

"Missiles?"

"No, sir. Just two sixteen-barreled rocket launchers."

"Flash a message to the frigate. Order them to cease fire immediately. Then give them a radio frequency we can use to talk."

"Yes, sir."

Colonel Cerilla spoke up. "Admiral, there's a speedboat heading toward us on the starboard side."

"All right," Crossley responded. There was no emotion in his voice. "We'll keep an eye on it."

Suddenly lights flashed all over the frigate as a salvo of shell went streaming toward the *Princess*, a deadly torrent of destruction. One by one the shells hit the ship and explosions rocked the sea. Fire broke out on the deck, fuel tanks exploded, and bodies were sent hurtling through the air. Some were seen jumping into the water, which was now ablaze from the spewing oil and fuel. All of the shells hit their mark, tearing the *Princess* and her equipment apart.

The officers and men of the American destroyer gazed in horror at the sight. Admiral Crossley mumbled something under his breath but continued to display no outward emotion.

By now the tender had reached the destroyer, and two sailors threw a rope ladder down to Denis and Jason, who was sobbing uncontrollably at the sight of the inflamed salvage ship. To Denis, the rippling Stars and Stripes overhead had never looked so good. "I've got to see the captain," Denis said as soon as he was taken on board.

On the bridge, the communications officer handed the admiral a microphone. "We've raised the frigate, sir," the officer said.

Admiral Crossley spoke into the microphone in a controlled voice. "Captain, this is Admiral Crossley of the United States Navy. I am placing you under arrest for an act of piracy and murder."

While he spoke, Colonel Cerilla saw a familiar face approach him. He recognized Denis Keyser instantly, despite the shapeless soggy clothes and the bleary eyes.

"Hello, Colonel," Denis said. "We meet in strange places, don't we?"

Cerilla did not acknowledge Denis' greeting but nodded to the sailor who had accompanied Denis, letting the sailor know that it was all right for the young man to remain on the bridge.

Admiral Crossley waited on the phone for a reply to his arrest order. He heard a discussion in Chinese, then a heavily accented voice spoke to him:

"We reject your arrest order, Admiral. You have no such rights. We claim the salvage site where we are now located in the name of the People's Republic of China. As for our so-called act of piracy, we inform you that the other vessel fired upon us first and we merely returned the fire in our own defense. There will be no further communication from our side." Crossley heard a click and the line went dead.

Now, for the first time, emotion showed in the admiral's expression as he faced his fellow officers. Denis was introduced by Colonel Cerilla and he gave a quick capsule version of what had taken place on the *Princess* and in the waters below.

"The Chinese claim that the *Princess* fired first," Crossley said.

"With what? BB guns? Those bastards just committed murder, Admiral." Denis raised his voice, and the strain showed through. "Are we going to let them get away with it?"

"Not if I can help it." Crossley turned to his executive officer, Commander Roland Haines, a third-generation naval officer and graduate of Annapolis. "Prepare a boarding party. We're going to board that Chinese ship."

"May I speak with you privately, sir?" Haines whispered.

The two men moved to the side of the bridge, out of earshot of the others.

Haines spoke in a low voice. "Admiral, I'm pretty well versed in international maritime conventions and laws. I spent three years in Naval Operations at the Pentagon. I thought maybe I should brief you before you made a final decision."

"What for?" Crossley bridled. "You saw what those bastards did."

"Yes, sir. But they claim the other vessel fired first, and we weren't close enough to witness it."

"The salvage ship was not armed, Commander."

"They had rifles, sir."

"Get to the point, Commander."

"I'm afraid, sir, that if we try to board the Chinese frigate, and they refuse to let us, they will have every right to fire on our men."

"And I'd have every right to fire back." Crossley was getting very annoyed at the younger officer. He turned and looked out to sea. The Chinese frigate was no more than two hundred yards away, dead in the water. On the frigate's deck, sailors scurried about, deeply involved in some kind of organized activity. Crossley wondered if they were about to begin a salvage operation of their own.

Haines's voice brought the admiral back to the immediate problem. "If we fire on them, sir, it would surely provoke an international incident. And I'm afraid we— and therefore the United States—would be at fault."

"Are you sure you know what you're talking about, Haines?"

"Yes, sir."

Crossley turned and stared at Haines. Is this what the Navy was coming to? What to Crossley was an obvious operational decision was being complicated by a litany of political and legal intricacies spewed from the mouth of a Naval Academy graduate. Crossley did not like this man at all. "Did it ever occur to you," he said, "that maybe you should have become a lawyer instead of a naval officer?"

"I'm sorry if my remarks have offended you, sir," Haines retorted soberly. "I feel it is my duty to share with you my knowledge of—"

"Well, you have," Crossley said. He walked back to the middle of the bridge, where the other officers, Colonel Cerilla, and Denis Keyser were standing.

Haines followed the admiral. "We could try to get through to the Pentagon, sir. They may want to call the White House on this. I was at the Pentagon during the *Pueblo* incident, and this could easily turn into—"

"Thank you, Commander," Crossley clipped. "I think I've been adequately briefed."

"One last thing, sir," Haines rejoined. "On your authority, we can file a formal protest through the State Department."

Denis had heard the last few exchanges and he seethed with anger he could no longer contain. "You'll do what? File a report? Those bastards out there have just murdered a bunch of Americans and all you can think of doing is file some goddamn report? I don't believe this!"

"Get him out of here!" Haines shouted.

"Let him stay," Admiral Crossley said calmly. He looked at Denis and spoke in a soft voice. "I appreciate your anger, young man. In fact, I feel exactly the same way you do about this sorry mess." Now Crossley turned around and stared out over the bow of his ship. To starboard lay the smoldering hull of the *Princess*. A rescue craft from the destroyer was on the site, picking up survivors. But there were not many. To port, the gray frigate stood still, a haughty murderer who disdained the policeman weak and powerless to do anything about the situation.

Admiral Crossley turned these thoughts over in his mind until his head ached. He was a man of simple virtues, but he had always defended his beliefs staunchly. He had just witnessed an act of piracy and cold-blooded mass murder, and all of his instincts and training told him to avenge the crimes. Legally, Haines contended, he could do nothing. But morally, what was he to do? Crossley would retire in a few years and head down to Sarasota, Florida, a place he loved dearly. Could he live with himself and the memory of this slaughter?

Crossley thought for a few more seconds and made his decision. There was no need to call the Pentagon. He already knew what their course of action would be. They'd check with the White House and come back with orders not to provoke an international incident. No, this was a decision Crossley had to make alone. And accept the consequences.

He rejected his initial idea of a boarding party. Haines was probably right about one thing: the Chinese might slaughter the American sailors. A different action was called for.

Crossley turned to the officers around him and said soberly: "Gentlemen, I'm sure you are as outraged as I am about the callous murders we have just witnessed. Haines has told me what the applicable diplomatic rules are, but I also know what justice is—or should be. Sometimes the rules set down by the politicians don't cover all the circumstances, and we have to make up our minds. Well, I've made my decision, and it is mine alone—I want everybody to be clear on that."

"What does all this mean, Admiral?" Denis asked.

Crossley allowed a faint smile. "It means, young man, that I am going to blow those fucking Chinese right out of the water."

The officers turned to one another and beamed broadly. Spirits were raised instantly by Crossley's announcement. Only Haines did not partake of the spirit of the moment. His face was sullen and pale. Before any one of them could say another word, Crossley began to bark the necessary orders.

"Sound general quarters! Prepare two Terrier missiles for launch."

"Aye, aye, sir!" came the enthusiastic reply.

"Target the Chinese frigate. And I want bull's-eyes!"

"Roger, sir."

On deck, the sleek Terrier missiles, fixed to their firing mechanisms, rotated into position for launch. Slowly, the missile transports rose, pointing skyward in the direction of the Chinese frigate.

Now Crossley prepared to give the final series of commands. Something held him back, that last vestige of doubt. He dismissed it from his mind and gave his order: "Commence launch sequence."

"Launch sequence commenced, sir."

"Trajectory."

"Entered. Locked."

"Telemetry."

"Entered."

"Arm missiles."

"Missiles armed, sir."

"Countdown to fire."

"Counting down from five at my mark, sir. . . . Mark."

"Five. Four. Three. Two. One. Fire!"

From their twin launchers on the foredeck two thin, gleaming white Terrier missiles soared off the pad heading skyward. All eyes on deck and on the bridge followed the missiles as they flew together, now clearly on a course that would take them to the Chinese frigate. In seconds the Terriers reached their apogee and, in tandem, arced downward on the second half of their deadly journey.

Across the water, a frenzy of activity swept through the frigate, once the missiles had been sighted. Little people scurried about, shouting, no doubt, and pointing to the sky. The gun turrets on the frigate rotated to face the American destroyer, but it was too late. The Terriers found their target easily and simultaneously struck the center of the Chinese vessel. An explosive roar tore through the atmosphere as the ship came apart in thousands of pieces. Smaller explosions succeeded one another, and fire engulfed the remains of the vessel. Bodies floated everywhere in the water, most of them lifeless.

On the destroyer's decks, dozens of sailors hooted and hollered exuberantly, waving their caps, showing their fists.

Justice had been served.

"Send a party out for survivors," Admiral Crossley ordered.

Colonel Cerilla stared at the man, wondering, no doubt, what he would have done in the same situation. The admiral had just put the finishing touch on his career. He would never again be entrusted with a command. At best, he would be allowed to retire prematurely.

The other officers on the bridge had gone off to their assigned duties, leaving only Colonel Cerilla, Denis Keyser, and Admiral Deke Crossley, who caught Cerilla staring at him.

"Anything wrong, Colonel?" Crossley asked.

"No, sir. I was just wondering."

"Wondering?"

"Yes, sir. I was wondering if, like you, I would have had the guts to do what was right."

chapter
24

"There were twelve survivors, Admiral," the lieutenant informed him. He had just returned from leading the rescue party to the site of the burnt-out Chinese frigate.

"Thank you, Sam," Crossley responded. His face showed the effects of the mental and emotional strain he had been subjected to. "What was the name of that spy? Peter Sloan?"

"Yes, Admiral," Denis replied. He had told Admiral Crossley and Colonel Cerilla about seeing Sloan on the deck of the frigate as she approached the *Princess*.

"Was Sloan among the survivors?" Crossley asked.

"There's a dark-haired, tall fellow, sir. Not in uniform, and he could easily pass for a Caucasian."

"That's him," Denis said.

"Well, get him on up here," Crossley ordered. "Colonel Cerilla and I want to have a chat with him."

"Can I sit in?" Denis asked. "I worked with him, and I can probably help with the—"

"Absolutely not!" Cerilla snapped. As an intelligence officer, he was confident that the admiral would not over-rule him on this point.

Denis was in no mood to be combative. He had just

witnessed the death of hundreds of men and the awesome destruction of two ships, and his stomach turned at the vivid recollection of the scenes. There were only four survivors, in addition to himself and Jason, from the *Princess*, so devastating had been the Chinese artillery attack. The salvage ship had simply disintegrated. Now Peggy was gone, Soapy was gone, Dr. Creuset was gone. All because of that bastard Sloan. Maybe it was better that Denis not sit in on the interrogation: he might tear Sloan limb from limb.

Denis felt a new attack of nausea overcome him, and he departed hurriedly. Soon after he left, Peter Sloan was escorted into the admiral's stateroom by two armed guards.

Sloan had been given fresh clothing, and did not appear battered or overcome by his experience of a few hours earlier when he had been pulled from the ocean. Crossley motioned to him to sit down at the end of a long table, with the guards flanking him, while Colonel Cerilla and Admiral Crossley took seats side by side, opposite their prisoner.

Admiral Crossley decided that Colonel Cerilla should conduct the interrogation, since he was a Pentagon intelligence officer. Crossley spoke crisply to Sloan, telling him who Colonel Cerilla was, reminding him of the severity of his actions.

Sloan acknowledged the comments with a nod, but gave the impression of a man who intended to say very little, if he said anything at all.

"Let me start by clearing the air on a few facts, Sloan," Colonel Cerilla said tersely. "First, we know that you are an agent of the People's Republic of China, that your mother is a high official in Peking, and that you have been operating as an agent in the United States for four years."

Sloan's face remained expressionless.

"Under the laws of the United States, if you are found guilty of treason—that's the charge, since you have a legitimate American passport because your father was American—you may be sentenced to death. In view of the countless lives lost as a result of your treachery, I fully intend to ask for the death penalty unless you cooperate with me to the fullest extent. Are you prepared to cooperate?"

Still, Sloan's face registered no emotion, and he did not respond.

"Very well," Cerilla continued in a businesslike tone, "since you do not wish to cooperate, I will request that Admiral Crossley exercise his prerogative of conducting the trial for treason here aboard the ship. If you are found guilty, there is no appeal, and you will be shot." Cerilla rose, the conversation apparently over. "Good day."

At that Peter Sloan's face suddenly came to life. "Wait. . . . You can't conduct a trial on this ship!"

"We can and we will. I'll be happy to show you the applicable code. There are several legal officers on board, and one will be assigned to your defense."

"No. Wait. Please," Sloan said in a voice full of tension.

Cerilla slowly sat down again. "I have some questions for you, Mr. Sloan. But I will not waste time beating around the bush. Do I make myself clear? Admiral Crossley can order your trial at any moment we feel that we are not getting your full cooperation."

"I understand," Sloan said, his head lowered.

Admiral Crossley observed the proceedings silently, admiring Colonel Cerilla's skills at handling the interrogation. The colonel was clearly in charge.

"How long have you been an agent of the Chinese?" Cerilla asked sternly.

"Four years, like you said," Sloan replied.

"How were you recruited?"

Sloan sighed. "Several years ago I was asked to visit my mother in China. I had been raised by an aunt, my father's sister, in Baltimore, and I had not seen my mother since I was a small boy. I knew almost nothing about my Chinese family prior to being asked to make the trip."

"Who asked you?"

"I don't know—really. Most of the arrangements were done over the phone. Anyway, I went one summer. Spent the whole summer in Peking. I found a great affinity with my mother and her relatives. I respected them, as others did. I learned of the great values placed on family attachments, and I admired the industriousness of the Chinese people. I felt genuinely at home with them. This went on for three summers.

"When I left Peking the third time, the United States was in the throes of the Watergate scandal, and my disillusionment was total. I committed myself to help the Chinese in any nonmilitary manner I could. My mission would be to help China economically and politically, leaving the military espionage to others, who were better qualified for it. I was nevertheless fully trained as an agent, and I accepted my role."

"Your most recent assignment was to find a *Sherman* survivor who could lead you to the wreck and the gold. Is that correct?"

"Yes."

"How did you go about it?"

"Well," Sloan began, relaxing a bit, "we really didn't have any way to get to a *Sherman* survivor through normal channels. We obviously couldn't go to the Pentagon, and any overt attempt by me or anyone else to uncover one of those men would be quickly discovered. So the *Sherman* plan was what you'd call a back-burner affair for a long time. Until Amelia Earhart, that is."

"Until you and your Chinese colleagues decided to plant an Amelia Earhart impersonator in Australia," Cerilla added, keeping up the pace of the narrative.

Suddenly Sloan appeared genuinely puzzled. He mulled over Cerilla's words for a few seconds, as if he had not clearly understood them, and finally spoke up: "We didn't plant that woman!"

Cerilla's face froze. Crossley coughed nervously. Both men stared at their prisoner, who stared back at them, a look of fear in his eyes.

"You remember what I told you about the trial?" Cerilla said menacingly.

"Colonel, I remember it very well, believe me. I'm telling you the truth. Although I have committed myself politically to China, I am not a fanatic. I'm afraid I enjoy life too much for that. And I'm bargaining for my life right now. I'm telling you, Colonel, the Chinese had nothing to do with that woman. I assumed she was real! Isn't she?"

Crossley and Cerilla looked at each other. Their eyes asked the same question.

Sloan continued, speaking quickly and nervously. "When Amelia Earhart came on the scene, I was given instructions to use her to get at a *Sherman* survivor. The plan was that once we found the *Sherman*, China would have a legitimate international claim on the gold. That's what I was told, anyway. I leaked the *Sherman* story to Denis Keyser, figuring that his article about gold on the *Sherman*—and subsequent articles after that—would bring forward any of the survivors who until then didn't know what their precious cargo had been. We assumed that the Pentagon never told them what was on the ship, so if any of the survivors remembered where the ship went down, he would have no incentive to speak up about it until he found out that there was a fortune on board. That is, of course, precisely what happened. Jason Caldwell came forward and tried to find the ship so he could claim the gold. My mission was to go along and find it too. Only, once it was found, we would claim it in the name of the People's Republic. If necessary, we were prepared to use force to get what belonged to us."

"The Earhart woman disappeared a few days ago. Are you telling me you knew nothing about that?"

"I didn't know it until this instant, Colonel. You must believe me."

Cerilla turned to Admiral Crossley. "With your permission, Admiral, I'll dismiss the prisoner."

Crossley nodded his assent.

"Take him below," Cerilla ordered. The two guards lifted Sloan unceremoniously and hauled him away.

When the two officers were alone, Crossley spoke first. "Well, what about Amelia Earhart, Colonel? Do you believe your prisoner?"

Cerilla let out a deep breath. "Yes, I believe him. He's confessed everything else. There would be no reason for him to lie about that part. Oh, we'll give him a lie-detector test eventually, but I'm sure the outcome will be the same. You were right, Admiral."

"About Earhart? Well, I just thought the idea of training a seventy-eight-year-old woman was a bit farfetched. By the way, I never heard any of those regulations about trials on board. Did you make that up?"

"Yes, sir. It's a routine ploy. Unless your prisoner is a fanatic or is unusually well-versed in the law, he's not going to take a chance on getting shot at sea." Cerilla's voice trailed off, and he stared at the ceiling.

"Something else bothering you, Colonel?"

Cerilla shook his head. "I was just wondering who that old woman could be."

chapter
25

On July 2, 1937, the following radio transmissions were the last received from Amelia Earhart by the cutter Itasca, which was monitoring her flight from Lae to Howland Island.

Earhart: "We must be on you but cannot see you. Gas is running low. Have been unable to reach you by radio. We are flying at one thousand feet."

Earhart: "We are circling but cannot see island. Cannot hear you. Go ahead on 7500 kHz with long counts either now or on schedule. Time on half hour."

Earhart: "Earhart calling Itasca. We received your signals but unable to get minimum. Please take bearings on us and answer on 3105 kHz."

Earhart: "We are on the line of position 157-337. Will repeat this message on 6210 kHz. We are running north and south."

No other messages from Amelia Earhart were heard.

Jason sat on the bunk in the cramped quarters, his face sullen, his eyes bloodshot and tired. Denis sat beside him trying as best he could to comfort the older man.

Jason finally got up the courage to ask the question, although he barely got it out. "Were there any other survivors?" he stammered.

"Only four, I'm afraid."

"Peggy?" Jason's eyes begged.

"I'm sorry, Jason. I really am."

"I should never have brought her here. . . ."

"Peggy was a big girl, Jason. She made her choice, right down to the last decision, which was to stay or come with us. She knew what she wanted. You had nothing to do with it."

The cabin door opened and Cerilla poked his head in. "I need to see you, Keyser," he said.

"I'm busy now, Colonel."

"It's urgent."

"Then come in and join us," Jason offered with a wave. "We've got no secrets anymore."

Cerilla walked in and closed the door behind him. "Matter of fact, I have business with both of you. You first, Keyser. I want to talk to you about your story."

Denis smiled wryly. "I've been trying to get you to do that for months."

Cerilla's expression remained serious. He sat in the only other empty chair and now faced Denis and Jason, who were also seated.

"The Secretary of Defense asked me to talk to you," Cerilla continued. "We're asking you not to publish the story of what happened here today. Likewise, Caldwell, I want a pledge of silence from you, too. If either of you speaks out—"

"Are you threatening again, Colonel?" Denis interrupted. "Have you been rummaging through my closets for more skeletons?"

Cerilla raised his hand, a gesture to ask Denis to calm down. "I'm not threatening you. I'm trying to reason with you. Hear me out, all right?"

"Go on," Denis said calmly.

Jason sat up and listened attentively while Cerilla resumed speaking.

"We've had a very serious military incident out here; you witnessed it yourself. A warship of the United States Navy sank a Chinese naval vessel in an act of war. Yes, I know we were justified, but that does not lessen the gravity of the incident." Cerilla took a deep breath. "It is the Secretary's opinion, as well as mine, that if the details of this incident can be kept secret, the Chinese and we would just as soon forget it ever happened."

"You're going to forget about those hundred or so people who died out there?"

"Keyser, please don't be so naive. Try to put this situation in the perspective of a possible global confrontation. We cannot afford to play brinksmanship with the Chinese. You know as well as I do that in any other country we would not even be having this discussion. You would be ordered not to print a word of what happened and that would be that."

"That's one of the things I like about our country, Colonel. Frankly, I prefer to see controls on the military, not free speech."

"Whatever our respective views," Cerilla continued evenly, "the end result comes down to this: you, Denis Keyser, have the power to write a story which could readily provoke a nuclear confrontation, and no one, not even the President of the United States, can legally stop you."

Denis stared at the Colonel for a moment, knowing that Cerilla was not prone to exaggeration. "Very heady stuff, Colonel. Very heady."

Cerilla continued, his voice as serious as before. "I need your pledge that you will not publish or discuss these events for at least five years."

"Don't rush me. I'll think about it."

"There's only one acceptable course of action you can follow, Keyser," Cerilla added with an edge.

"You're threatening again."

Cerilla hesitated a second before speaking. "Look at it this way. I have the responsibility to protect the interests of the United States in this situation. I'm not certain you understand the very real dangers involved here. If it comes to using information I may know about your background to stop you from provoking an international crisis, I'll do it."

"That, Colonel, is a blatant threat."

"Oh, come off it, Keyser! You whining liberals make me sick. Here we are equating your selfish desire to write an ego-inflating story that the world can easily live without, with the possibility of a global confrontation with the Chinese. Under those circumstances, of course I'll try to stop you!"

"Sure. With blackmail, threats, and any other dirty tricks you can use to get your way. Right, Colonel? Say, off the record, will I have to watch out for dark alleys?"

Cerilla shook his head in disgust. Jason had not uttered a word during the exchange with Denis. Now Cerilla turned his attention to the older man.

"What did you expect to get out of this expedition, Caldwell?" Cerilla asked.

Jason shrugged. "The gold, of course."

"Did it occur to you," Cerilla continued, "that the gold is the property of the United States government? There is no statute of limitations on ownership in cases like this."

Denis shook his head. "Oh, for Christ's sake, Cerilla. You didn't have a chance of finding that gold if it hadn't been for Caldwell."

"Need I remind you," the Colonel rejoined, "that if we hadn't been on the scene, your Chinese friends might have dealt with you rather differently. Would you have pressed your claim with them?"

Jason's voice quivered. "I found that gold."

"But you don't own it," Cerilla retorted. "You can, of course, take your case to court."

"I will," Jason said. But it was all academic; he could not afford a lengthy court battle.

"In researching the subject of lost government property, however," Cerilla continued, "we did learn that the government, occasionally and entirely at its own discretion, awards finder's fees to persons who are instrumental in recovering lost or stolen government property."

Denis and Jason's attention perked up.

Cerilla chose his words carefully. "There are a number of precedents," he went on, "but no specific rules. It's entirely a judgment call, so to speak."

Denis looked Cerilla in the eye. "I smell a bribe, Colonel."

"I thought you might take it that way, but that's your problem. The Secretary believes that you will both do your duty as responsible citizens and not reveal the story of the *Sherman* and what happened here. In turn, the Department of Defense will take a liberal view of your role in finding the *Sherman*, and you will be granted a finder's fee of one percent of the value of the recovered property. To be specific, that's a total of five million dollars."

"And if I print the story?"

"Then no finder's fee. You have no legal claim to it."

"So if I don't go along, Jason gets screwed."

"Correct."

The expression on Jason's face left little doubt that it would be an easy decision for him. "You're entitled to at least half the money, Denis," Jason said. "You saved my life."

"I didn't come out here for the money. I came here to do a story."

Jason sighed. "It's your decision."

Denis rose and opened the cabin door. "I'm going for a walk on deck."

The destroyer heaved slightly and the strong wind filled Denis' lungs and rustled through his hair. He held the railing and stared out to sea, wishing that Sacha could be there. He missed her most after they had been separated a few days, and especially now as he faced an awesome moral decision.

Denis reviewed the issues in his mind. A reporter's first obligation is to the story. That's what freedom of the press is all about. But Cerilla's arguments about the possibility of a global confrontation were chillingly realistic and plausible.

Out of the corner of his eye Denis saw Colonel Cerilla walking along the deck, heading toward him.

"I know it's not an easy decision for you," Cerilla said in a conciliatory tone. He came alongside, and both men gazed out to sea.

Denis acknowledged the colonel's comment with a nod.

"I think Jason wants to talk to you," Cerilla added.

"Yeah. I'm sure he does." Denis thought for a moment. "You really believe that business about the nuclear confrontation with the Chinese, don't you?"

"I have many reasons to believe it. Reasons I can't share with you."

Denis turned and looked squarely at Cerilla. "I'm prepared to withhold the story, Colonel. But there's a condition."

"I can't sweeten the offer, if that's what you mean."

"Forget the money. It belongs to Jason, anyway. I want something different. My court-martial records at the Pentagon. I want the slate wiped clean."

"Agreed."

The two men looked at one another for a moment, and Cerilla offered his hand. They shook hands, then walked along the deck toward the bow.

"Jason will insist you get some of the money," Cerilla said matter-of-factly.

Now that he had made his decision, Denis felt almost serene; a cumbersome weight had been lifted from him. "I decided a long time ago that I wasn't destined to be rich. It would only corrupt me."

"I can easily understand that," Cerilla commented.

Denis grinned. "But maybe just this once, I'll let a little corruption seep through."

Both men laughed for a moment, then they walked a little farther in silence until Cerilla spoke again.

"Amelia Earhart disappeared, Denis. She walked right out of the hospital and never returned."

Denis stared at Cerilla in disbelief. "When?"

"A few days ago. We thought she was part of the Chinese scheme but we don't think so any more."

"I always thought she was real," Denis said. "I could almost feel it."

As they continued their walk, Denis replayed in his mind the coast-to-coast search he and Sacha had made for the clues to the Earhart-*Sherman* mystery. It had been exhilarating even though Denis never proved that Mrs. Stenemond was really Amelia Earhart.

"You know, Colonel," Denis said, "a long time ago, I asked you what you thought of Amelia Earhart but you evaded the question."

Cerilla thought for a moment before replying. "I spent almost an entire career on Amelia Earhart, Denis, and I feel I know her intimately. You can imagine my shock when one of the impostors turned out to have information only Earhart herself possessed."

"What's your opinion about Mrs. Stenemond, Colonel? Not the official version—your own."

Cerilla paused, then said, "My private opinion is that Emily Stenemond is in fact Amelia Earhart. But I'm afraid she's had her fill of us, the investigators, the greedy doctors, the journalists, the whole lot. I don't think we'll ever see her again."

They were close to the bow of the ship. Denis stopped and leaned against the railing. "I guess we finally agree on something, Colonel," Denis said. "I don't think she'll be back either, and for Emily Stenemond's sake, I think we ought to leave it at that. But I wonder if I'll be able to resist the temptation to try to find her."

ABOUT THE AUTHOR

PETER TANOUS is Chairman of the Board of Petra Capital Corporation, a New York-based international investment banking firm. Previously, he was associated with a major Wall Street stock brokerage firm where he was responsible for overseas branch offices. Mr. Tanous was raised in Paris and New York and travels frequently to Europe and the Middle East. His first novel, *The Petrodollar Takeover* (co-authored with Paul Rubinstein), was published in 1975.